THE TABLE OF

Contents

Contents

FANTASY FOOTBALL 2023

Introduction

Football, the beloved spectacle of North America, ignites passions far and wide. Enter Fantasy Football—an artful dance of strategy and camaraderie. While not the traditional pitch-and-tackle, excelling as a virtual maestro bestows accolades, respect, and even treasures. From die-hard enthusiasts to the casual wanderer, everyone envisions the zenith, predicting victors and standouts with fervor. The less initiated may rely on geographic happenstance and jersey hues for their allegiance. Yet, it's the fusion of knowledge, shrewd tactics, and that indescribable gut feeling that ignites the magic—a tapestry of bonds among comrades and pals.

Embarking on this odyssey, like life's grand endeavors, demands constancy. This book is your compass to navigate the labyrinth of fantasy football. Following these methods with unwavering consistency ensures triumph over your weekly rivals. For novices and veterans alike, the tome infuses confidence, wisdom, and prosperity. So, venture forth and harness the thrill of the gridiron spectacle—may it bring you joy, camaraderie, and a league-topping journey. Your fantasy saga begins here.

Unveiling the Puzzle

Fantasy Football Dynamics

In the realm of fantasy football, destiny unfurls before NFL players even grace the turf. It's a calculated game, a blend of numbers, logic, and the quirks that define each unique league. As the sun kisses August skies, know this — the war isn't won during those grueling twice-daily training sessions. The secret lies in strategizing well before expert-generated spreadsheets and player rankings surface.

The mission? Outsmart fellow fans, amassing a crescendo of fantasy points forged from real-life gridiron performances. The lineup canvases multiple NFL dimensions: quarterbacks, running backs, wide receivers, tight ends, kickers, and sometimes the bold guardians of defense. A symphony of fantasy leagues convenes in weekly showdowns, tabulating touchdowns and yards into a symphony of points, crowning the victor with the highest score.

The league's heartbeat resonates in records and playoff stakes. The victor emerges crowned by the best record or a top-tier playoff seed. Comprising ten to twelve squads, each league ventures into a draft battleground, battling uncertainty round after round to fortify their ranks. The team's architecture is the architect of its triumph.

Now, as the digital age dawns, fantasy football aficionados pore over the cryptic scrolls of expert advice found in magazines, online realms, and even televised debates. Yet, amidst the sea of "underrated" labels and pundit rankings, a truth dawns — everyone's leafing through the same tome. In a universe of statistical forecasts and projections, seizing the upper hand rests on your capacity to decipher data in ways that eclipse the masses.

The journey of fantasy football thrives on dissecting complexity, summoning strategic finesse, and painting your victory upon the canvas of the gridiron. May your analysis bloom brighter, your insights stand taller, and your triumphs resonate louder in this captivating saga!

Tactics And Strategies

In the intricate tapestry of fantasy football drafting, envision a realm of twelve contenders vying for glory each week. As the field changes, so do your adversaries. Yet, the spotlight is on your soldiers, their feats etched against your rivals'. Remember, it's not just about the total score; it's the distribution that wields true might. Your week two foe might bring a bigger arsenal than week one. Uniform wins demand no exaggerated victories—look for players to outshine feeble NFL defenses your opponents employ.

Note 1: As we embark on this journey, let's acknowledge the dearth of an infallible playbook for handpicking the perfect player for your ensemble. Craftsmanship that guarantees a powerhouse team, the veritable phoenix of weekly matchups, is no simple feat. The complexities confound mere paper calculations. Still, fret not, for strategies abound to fortify your odds of triumph.

Note 2: This primer, while tailored for novices of fantasy sports, presumes a modicum of football acumen. Rules that govern the gridiron's dance will find no mention within these pages

For the NFL aficionados who embrace the world of money leagues, here's the playbook for boosting your odds.

Building Your Budget Playbook

Game on, fellow NFL aficionados! Your game plan? Set those weekly and seasonal budgets in stone, whether it's a cool $100,000 or a humble $10. If you're a rookie in the realm of real-money fantasy, practice is your North Star. Remember, it's like anything else: the more you dive in, the more you'll grasp. Over time, you'll master the intricacies of matchups and leagues you partake in. So, lay down the law with both a weekly and seasonal budget, then sprinkle that budget magic according to your contests and lineups.

Tip: Make your first deposit match your initial season budget. Now, divvy up that weekly budget among various contests or game types. Explore diverse game options, embrace the thrill of competing against varying buy-ins and players. For example, if you're rocking a $100 weekly budget, join five to ten games a week. Expect wins and losses—it's all part of the journey. Don't waver from your long-term strategy and weekly budget.

Here's the kicker—refrain from reinvesting your winnings all season. Cash out those winnings, and stick to your initial seasonal budget. Now, here's the catch—practice isn't free. Freerolls are fun, but the real game-changer? Dabbling in every competition flavor. Set aside a practice game budget of at least $150. But hey, don't go all-in, okay? Keep your stakes between 20 to 25% of your fund in any given week.

Ready to step up your fantasy game? It's time to flex those budgeting muscles and turn practice into prowess!

Maximum Yardage: Deposit Your Passion for the NFL

For novice NFL fantasy enthusiasts, it's common to seek immediate rewards. That alluring deposit bonus is a one-time gig, but it's a patient dance till it lands in your real account. Embrace a marathon mindset — let that bonus and initial deposit nurture a long-haul vision. Nearly every fantasy league doubles your initial deposit, just once. You're here to conquer, signifying a season of many showdowns. Aim for the stars — go big on your first deposit for that splendid money match. Newbies are known for their caution, dipping their toes before the plunge into regular deposits. Mastery demands practice to uncover your winning mix of formula, strategy, and challenges. If your wallet permits, go all in for that mammoth opening deposit, priming yourself for a fruitful voyage. Remember, withdrawing is an option, but seize your chance for that golden money match. You've got one shot — make it count!

Dive into the NFL's Tapestry

"For fellow NFL enthusiasts, let's dive into the gridiron of fantasy leagues! Every league is a unique ballgame, each with its own scoring and rules. Wingin' it won't cut it. Before the showdown begins, invest a mere ten minutes to decipher the league's scoring, settings, and contest nuances. Why? Because these gems hold the key to those coveted points. Picture this: passing touchdowns might be a cool 4 points, but a rushing TD could be a majestic 6. Get familiar with the playbook before taking the field.

Here's the lowdown on some game-changing settings:
1) Roster Roaming: Some leagues slam the door once rosters are set, while others keep it ajar. Beware of the roster-locking league; it could throw a wrench in your lineup if games and trades get the boot.
2) Winning Positions: Know how many spots on the roster will get you the moolah. 50/50 matchups sweet-talk the top fifty percent with a fixed amount, while grand tournaments crown only a handful of heavy hitters. The game plan for a million-dollar faceoff against 5,000 contenders is as different as chalk and cheese from a fifty-player 50/50 showdown.

So here's the drill: Get your playbook straight for each league, eye the risks, and then roll those dice with your winning roster."

From Practice to Perfection

Here's the playbook for victory: Practice, my fellow NFL devotees, is your true MVP. Take the field in low-stake skirmishes before tackling the big league's $2,000 game. Eye the masters in $2 head-to-head battles atop the leaderboard; unravel their drafting wizardry. Bet you'll spot some unexpected players on their roster. Newbies often draft from the heart, and while passion plays its part, don't let it steer your ship entirely. Your roster isn't just an all-star gala; treasure troves of consistent performers lead the way. Before unleashing your treasure chest, sample each contest at least five times, like dipping your toes in different rivers before you dive. Freerolls? They're like appetizers—tasty, but not always packed with the finest foes. Seek out formidable opponents, those whose lineups clash against yours, like gladiators in the arena. Soon, you'll sense a rhythm, a melody in the type of players you seek. This, my friends, is the art of crafting a gridiron empire.

Create your personal lineup away from the digital realm

"For those of you diving into fantasy football for the first time or seasoned vets looking to up your game, listen up. Navigating the digital draft realm can be like wandering into a carnival of stars, lights flashing and chat streaming. It's both thrilling and overwhelming. But wait, here's a tip: go old-school with offline roster creation. Block out the noise, gather your resources, and decipher the metrics. You've got the scoop on level one vs. level two players. Dump those salary stats into Excel and let the magic unfold. Now, build your system. Handpick those tier-two wonders, add a sprinkle of metrics, and voila—a value system emerges. Do the same for your top-tier superstars. Mind you, a diverse roster's key to victory, given the league you're in. Safeguarded stars hog your budget, so be shrewd. Seek those hidden gems with the appetite for success. The journey might twist and turn, but once you've honed in, you're ahead. Vet your value picks, sidestepping distractions. Stay anchored to your offline playbook during drafting. Remember, your league's "My Account" is a treasure trove of wisdom. Study your past battles, crunch numbers, and fine-tune your strategy. Unearth the unsung heroes, and soon patterns emerge. One day, you'll dance with delight as your unique picks shine. Save and archive, for this tale of triumph deserves a place in your fantasy football saga."

Resources and Research in NFL Fantasy

This chapter, often shoved into the shadows, emerges as the unsung hero of victory. Ignored for its time-consuming nature, it carries hidden joys and thrilling challenges. Picture it as a treasure hunt, a quest for top talent at a value that packs a punch. Your quest? To seize the metrics edge over your rivals, a pivotal step in the path to sustained triumph. Now, if you're up for a mere money-spending spree and a casual romp, feel free to skip this stage, pick your league favorites, and forget the stats and matchups. But if your eyes are set on fortune, then buckle up for the ride of research, crafting, and refinement.

This journey is a symphony of trial and error, composing a research strategy. Start by assembling a lineup of metrics you sense as game-changers. Think matchups — a common starting point. Who's got the weakest defense against passing? Which players feast on the most porous pass defense? Track points dropped by opponents, the yards reaped by tight ends, running backs, and receivers. Dive into the game's context — location, circumstances — to gauge the opponent's strategy. Factor in injuries, decode your rival's weaknesses. As you tick off the stats you've conquered, a bespoke research pattern takes shape. With each game, you polish your unique metrics.

Ah, the middle-tier gems that often tip the scales! Keep a hawk-eye on offensive injuries, especially in run-heavy schemes. Ready to snag a backup RB from a ground game-crazy outfit? With a well-planned strategy in place and a consistent approach, researching becomes a breeze. Armed with direction, research transforms from a daunting chore into an exhilarating adventure. Trust me, when you know your goals and are prepped, the journey becomes smoother, swifter, and dare I say, fun.

Gear up to align your game plan, outline your research needs, and steer towards the right resources. No need to reinvent the wheel to identify the defense leaking those passing TDs. Someone's done the analytical legwork; you just need to unearth the data. Expert pick platforms backed by stats or direct data sleuthing, the choice is yours. While everyone's eyeing the big players, sneak deeper into the game. Yahoo Sports, FFToolbox, Bleacher Report, ESPN, and Fantasy Pros get a rookie's nod. But to truly ascend, you must venture further, beyond the beaten track.

Riding the coattails of common wisdom often leaves you in the shadows. The web's brimming with specialized fantasy havens brimming with insights. If you're tempted by the easy route, steer clear of the mentioned analysis haunts. Plenty of sites offer weekly value picks, some even flaunt a value score for specific Daily Sports fantasy leagues. Most resource sites thrive on affiliations, nudging traffic towards conventional fantasy platforms. They fixate on one money league, sidelining others. However, the real game-changers exploit data feeds from multiple leagues, crafting projections that align with reality.

So, build your game plan, hunt those resources, and dive deep into your research. Disregarding this phase? Well, expect to find yourself mired in the bottom 25% of every contest. Your voyage to victory begins here!

Craft your picks guided by your data

Game on, NFL fans! Different leagues, different strategies—got it? Before you dive into drafting, let data be your compass, no matter the league. Embrace a model mindset; ditch the "winging it" notion. Your wins will soar on data wings, even if it curbs the thrill.

Historic stats? A dime a dozen. But hold up, champ. Building an edge takes more steps. Got a player facing a specific team? Expand your view—compare similar players. Season and career length limit data, but your analysis shouldn't be. Keep your focus on the now—don't fixate on last year's feats. Fresh, updated intel is your weapon. Your goal? Spot the diamonds others miss. That's where victory hides, no matter the league style.

Value picks—crucial game changers. Build a system that pumps out high-value projections, and you're drafting with data's beat. Imagine this: an emotional drafter's itching for Calvin Johnson. Hold on—forking over your cash for a superstar spikes your risk. With Johnson's bill paid, can your roster still dance? Doubtful. Data's your ace. Say you've got Larry Fitzgerald at 21.6 and Keenan Allen at 19.4—voila, 41 points! The system rules. Sure, not every draw will be this sweet, but data-driven drafts often have you leading the pack.

Leagues set the stage. Tourneys? Risk lovers unite. Two to three 1st tier players are your gems. Scout wisely—don't shower cash on duds. Others might nab similar gems; your magic's in those value picks. Check this out: 2nd Tier QBs match 1st Tier RBs but might deliver more points. The data-unicorn whispers your choices.

As you climb the drafting ladder, data relevance dawns. Keep emotions on mute, stay true to your process. Draft based on your data dance and unveil the value kings!

Keep an eye out for the latest news

"NFL fans, brace yourselves for a strategic curveball! Drafting your fantasy team well in advance might seem tempting, but hold your horses. From cancellations to trades, weather quirks to personal dramas, and even legal hiccups—oh, the NFL drama knows no bounds! Picture this: you're in a million-dollar showdown, and that star player you drafted is benched due to an unforeseen injury. Ouch, right? Don't let laziness trump your chances! Keep tabs, make wise choices, and stay on top of the game. After all, why let a moment's negligence tarnish your quest for victory?"

Select the appropriate competition

In the realm of NFL fantasy, your choice of contest wields the power to build your fortune or erode your coffers. Within the NFL's tapestry, diverse contests emerge, hinging on their leagues' nuances. Yet, a common thread weaves through most—an array of offerings for the discerning strategist. Immerse yourself in myriad contests, traversing the landscape from $1 to $0, crafting your craft. Enlist in H2H bouts against leader board luminaries, treading cautiously with a modest dollar or two. Delve into the crucible, acquainting yourself with pay structures, drafting nuances, and multifarious formats. The crux? Each contest deserves its unique playbook, a symphony of strategy. As you plunge into the multi-game mosaic, a resonance shall stir within you—a penchant for certain contests. Seek your match, your muse. Then, my friend, it's time to dissect, analyze, and tailor-make a blueprint of triumph for your chosen battleground.

Select your adversary

"Calling all NFL fanatics! Dive into the realm of fantasy with a strategic twist. Certain fantasy platforms offer glimpses into user triumphs and track records across sports. Decode fellow users, aim with precision. When your stakes are high, evading the top-tier grinders on leaderboards is essential. Harness your data to cherry-pick opponents, and scout these adept players on RotoGrinders.com, where their monikers gleam across fantasy money leagues. Steer clear of the top 25 to 50 contenders. Proficient fantasy grinders thrive across contests, but their consistent victories blossom in H2H duels. These virtuosos, led by the likes of super grinder Condia, can juggle up to 20 battles a day. Yet, surrendering 18 to 20 matches to a grinder isn't exactly a thrill ride. Dodge leaderboard dominators. When crafting H2H matchups, tread cautiously, as these grinders scoop up contests like candy. Save crafting leagues for the proven pros. Opt for H2H encounters with newcomers, fewer victories, and a short track record. It's a blast to dance in grand payout showdowns, but think of it as more of a lottery than a calculated venture. Embrace the art of finding contests and matchups that sing to your strengths. If you're two contenders away from sealing a 10-player showdown, invest five minutes delving into their histories. Scrutinize the contests, uncover paths that tame your risk. Then, craft a tailor-made playbook for every contest flavor. Ready to rumble?"

Summon luck

The essence boils down to this: harness the power of top-tier resources and a methodical approach to curtail risk. Yet, in this grand tapestry of strategy, moments shall arise when luck beckons, and your gut speaks louder than any stat. Elevating your analytical prowess is akin to donning an MVP cape. However, the gridiron is a learning curve, and contenders evolve. Your personal touch, the subjective twist you add, holds the key. Amid unchanging variables—competition, methodology, tools, and data—your trump card remains the acumen to foresee victorious stars, a shade better than the rest. Lady Luck's sway hinges on your battleground, but plotting mitigates loss odds and fortune's sway. As the dust settles, your coffers burgeon through fantasy football finesse.

Crafting a Formula to Assemble a Victorious Fantasy Lineup

Much like crafting a delectable recipe, the essence lies in the ingredients, yet the alchemy demands more than a mere assembly. Akin to a culinary symphony, individual elements must harmonize. Enter your daily fantasy lineups—a canvas to orchestrate brilliance. Unravel the quest for perfection, where gifted athletes coalesce, birthing fantasy points. Brace for a journey through the realms of triumphant lineups, where high floors and tantalizing ceilings reign supreme. For cash game aficionados, a dash of upside serves well; tournaments, a hearty helping. Embrace the thrill of risk, for therein lies glory. Amidst it all, the salary cap—a canvas for your gridiron masterpiece.

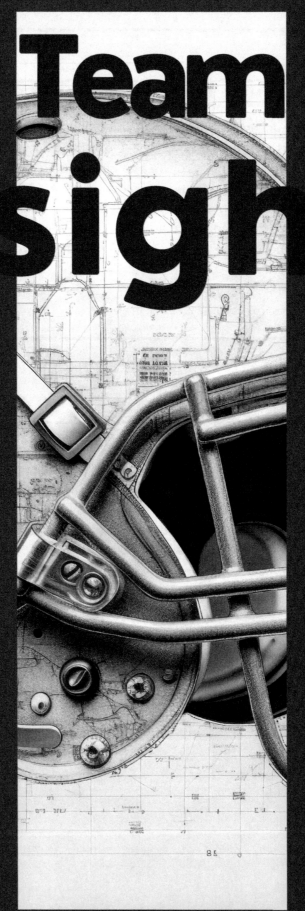

Key Losses

Team Insights

NFL Draft
Depth Chart
Schedule

Key Additions
& New
Contracts

Understanding the Arizona Cardinals' Strategy in NFL Fantasy Football

1. **Passing Focus:** The Cardinals prefer throwing the ball, led by Kyler Murray, a versatile quarterback excelling in both passing and running. Murray's accuracy at 66.7% enhances his impact.

2. **Receiver Strength:** DeAndre Hopkins leads a skilled receiver group. He's among the best in the league, a threat for game-changing plays. The team also has Christian Kirk, A.J. Green, and Marquise Brown, all capable of big plays.

3. **Running Game:** While not as strong as their passing, they can still run. James Conner leads the running game, tough between the tackles. Chase Edmonds is versatile, capable of running and catching passes.

4. **Team Philosophy:** Cardinals focus on scoring and winning. They take calculated risks to get their stars the ball and actively seek opportunities.

5. **Offensive Approach:** Tailored to Murray's strengths, they use play-action passes, designed runs, and quick passes to exploit his dual-threat ability.

Key Fantasy Picks for Your Team:

- Kyler Murray: A must-have due to his dual-threat prowess and accuracy in passing.
- DeAndre Hopkins: An elite receiver, always a big-play potential.
- Christian Kirk: A versatile, reliable receiver, great target for Murray.
- A.J. Green: An experienced player still capable of game-changing plays.
- Marquise Brown: Known for speed and deep threats, a valuable option.
- James Conner: A strong runner who can also catch passes, great for your team's running back needs.

Remember, the Cardinals aim to score and win, leaning on their pass-first strategy led by the talented Murray and a mix of explosive receivers.

Arizona Cardinals' run-pass tendencies in the 2022 NFL season

Play Type	Percentage
Passing plays	62.06%
Rushing plays	37.94%

Key Additions & New Contracts

Player	Position	Contract	Key Addition	Impact on Team
Kyzir White	LB	2 years, $11 million	Free agent signing	Provides much-needed depth at linebacker and could start alongside Isaiah Simmons
Hjalte Froholdt	OL	2 years, $3 million	Free agent signing	Provides depth on the offensive line and could compete for a starting job at guard
Kevin Strong	DT	1 year, $1.5 million	Free agent signing	Provides depth on the defensive line and could contribute as a rotational player
Marquise Brown	WR	3 years, $39 million	Trade from Baltimore Ravens	Provides a deep threat for Kyler Murray and takes pressure off DeAndre Hopkins

Key Losses

Position	Player
Wide receiver	DeAndre Hopkins
Tight end	Zach Ertz
Defensive end	Chandler Jones
Linebacker	Jordan Hicks
Cornerback	Byron Murphy Jr.

NFL Draft 2023

Round	Pick	Position	College	Player	Fantasy Projection
1	3	OT	Ohio State	Paris Johnson Jr.	120
2	41	DE	Florida	BJ Ojulari	110
3	72	CB	Alabama	Garrett Williams	90
4	105	RB	Iowa State	Breece Hall	100
5	168	WR	TCU	Quentin Johnston	80
6	180	CB	Louisville	Kei'Trel Clark	70
6	213	TE	Coastal Carolina	Isaiah Likely	60

Pos	Player	Why chosen
QB	Kyler Murray	The Cardinals have no need to draft a quarterback in the first round. Murray is a franchise quarterback and he is under contract for the next four years.
WR	Marquise Brown	Brown is a good wide receiver who can stretch the field. He is a good fit for the Cardinals' offense, which is led by Kyler Murray.
OT	Paris Johnson Jr.	The Cardinals need to improve their offensive line. Johnson is a good pass blocker and he has the potential to be a franchise left tackle.
CB	Garrett Williams	The Cardinals need to improve their secondary. Williams is a good cover corner and he has the potential to be a starter in the Cardinals' defense.

ARIZONA CARDINALS
2023 SEASON SCHEDULE

PRESEASON

| AUG. 11 ■ 7:00 PM | AUG. 19 ■ 5:00 PM | AUG. 26 ■ 10:00 AM |

REGULAR SEASON

| SEP. 10 ■ 10:00 AM | SEP. 17 ■ 1:05 PM | SEP. 24 ■ 1:25 PM | OCT. 1 ■ 1:25 PM | OCT. 8 ■ 1:05 PM |

| OCT. 15 ■ 1:25 PM* | OCT. 22 ■ 1:05 PM* | OCT. 29 ■ 1:25 PM* | NOV. 5 ■ 11:00 AM* | NOV. 12 ■ 2:05 PM* |

BYE WEEK

| NOV. 19 ■ 11:00 AM* | NOV. 26 ■ 2:05 PM* | DEC. 3 ■ 11:00 AM* | | DEC. 17 ■ 2:05 PM* |

SEAT GEEK

| DEC. 24 ■ 2:25 PM* | DEC. 31 ■ 11:00 AM* | WEEK 18 ■ TBD* | | |

HOME   AWAY   ALL TIMES MST (AZ)   *SUBJECT TO FLEXIBLE SCHEDULING

ATLANTA FALCONS

Understanding the Atlanta Falcons' NFL fantasy football dynamics

1. **Passing Power:** Falcons are all about the pass, led by QB Marcus Mariota, who excels in throwing and running. He's accurate too, with a 62.8% completion rate.
2. **Talented Receivers:** Calvin Ridley is a top-tier receiver, explosive every time he gets the ball. Other stars like Drake London, A.J. Brown, and Russell Gage also shine.
3. **Running Game:** Their running isn't as strong, but Cordarrelle Patterson stands out, being a good runner and pass-catcher.
4. **Team Approach:** Falcons want points and wins, unafraid to take risks to get their playmakers involved.
5. **Strategy:** They use Mariota's versatility with play-action passes, runs, and quick throws to create opportunities.
6. **Fantasy Picks:** Consider Mariota, Ridley, London, Brown, Gage, and Patterson for your team. They offer diverse strengths.
7. **Offensive Tactics:** Watch for play-action to trick defenses and quick throws to utilize their playmakers' skills.
8. **After-Catch Strategy:** Since their O-line isn't as strong, they rely on receivers to shine after catching the ball.
9. **2023 Outlook:** Falcons are on the rise, aiming for balance with good offseason moves.

Play Type	Percentage
Passing plays	61.9%
Rushing plays	38.1%

2022 Falcons:
- Favored passing plays (61.9% vs. 62.06% league average). Running game decent, averaged 4.0 yards per carry and 128.8 rushing yards per game.

Why Pass-First:
- Young QB Mariota, strong both in passing and running.
- Good wide receivers like Ridley and London.
- Offensive line allowed 46 sacks (10th most).

2023 Shift:
- New coach Arthur Smith, likes to run.
- May aim for a more balanced playstyle, depending on improved offensive line.

Key Additions & New Contracts

Player	Position	Contract	Key Addition/New Contract	Impact on Team
Trevor Reid	Offensive Tackle	3 years, $27 million	New Contract	Reid is a young and talented offensive tackle who should solidify the Falcons' offensive line.
Josh Ali	Wide Receiver	1 year, $1.7 million	Key Addition	Ali is a speedy wide receiver who can be a threat to stretch the field.
Ra'Shaun Henry	Running Back	1 year, $1.5 million	Key Addition	Henry is a powerful running back who can run between the tackles.
B.J. Hill	Defensive Tackle	3 years, $24 million	Key Addition	Hill is a strong and disruptive defensive tackle who can help improve the Falcons' run defense.

Key Losses

Position	Player
Wide Receiver	Calvin Ridley
Defensive End	Dante Fowler Jr.
Linebacker	Foye Oluokun
Safety	Duron Harmon
Cornerback	Fabian Moreau

NFL Draft 2023

Round	Pick	Position	College	Player	NFL Fantasy Projection
1	8	WR	Ohio State	Jaxon Smith-Njigba	100
2	43	OT	Central Michigan	Bernhard Raimann	80
3	74	CB	Washington	Kyler Gordon	70
4	114	RB	Alabama	Brian Robinson Jr.	60
5	154	LB	Georgia	Nakobe Dean	50
6	185	S	Penn State	Jalen Carter	40
7	228	DT	Georgia	Devonte Wyatt	30

Pos	Player	Why chosen
QB	Malik Willis	The Falcons need a quarterback and Willis has the potential to be a franchise quarterback.
WR	Jameson Williams	The Falcons need a wide receiver and Williams is a big-play threat who can take the top off of defenses.
OT	Charles Cross	The Falcons need an offensive tackle and Cross is a good pass blocker who can protect the quarterback.
CB	Kyler Gordon	The Falcons need a cornerback and Gordon is a good cover corner who can defend the pass.

2023 SCHEDULE

16

A Ground-Pounding Squad with a Versatile Quarterback

The Ravens focus on running the ball, led by Lamar Jackson, their quarterback who excels at both passing and running. He's also pretty accurate, completing about 64.1% of his throws.

Their running back crew is strong, with J.K. Dobbins as the speedy guy and Gus Edwards as the powerful one.

Their passing game is decent, not amazing. They've got fast Marquise Brown and big Rashod Bateman as key receivers.

The Ravens' main strategy is controlling the game clock and keeping their opponents' offense off the field. This means running the ball a lot and playing good defense.

They design their offensive plays around Jackson's dual skills. They mix in trick plays and quick throws to their playmakers.

All in all, the Ravens are a run-focused team with a young, skilled quarterback. They've got good running backs and a decent passing game. Their goal is to dominate time possession and win games.

For your fantasy football team, consider these players:
- Lamar Jackson: A must-have. He's a dual-threat quarterback, really accurate too.
- J.K. Dobbins: Great for fantasy teams needing a running back who can also catch.
- Marquise Brown: Perfect if you need a speedy receiver.
- Rashod Bateman: A solid choice if you want a receiver who can make big plays.

In 2022, the Ravens leaned heavily towards the run, with rushing plays at 53.7%, higher than the league average. Their passing game was decent, averaging 232.1 yards, while rushing averaged 190.7 yards per game.

Play Type	Percentage
Passing plays	46.3%
Rushing plays	53.7%

This approach was fueled by:
- Lamar Jackson's versatile skills
- Strong running back duo: J.K. Dobbins and Gus Edwards
- Exceptional offensive line

Expect the same trend in 2023 under new coach Mike Macdonald, known for prioritizing the run game.

Key Additions & New Contracts

Player	Position	Contract	Key Addition	Impact on Team
Odell Beckham Jr.	Wide Receiver	1 year, $1.5 million	Key Addition	Beckham is a former All-Pro receiver who can provide a big boost to the Ravens' passing game.
Nelson Agholor	Wide Receiver	1 year, $1.25 million	Key Addition	Agholor is a solid receiver who can play outside or in the slot. He will help to fill the void left by Marquise Brown.
Geno Stone	Safety	2 years, $3 million	New Contract	Stone is a versatile safety who can play in the box or in coverage. He will help to solidify the Ravens' secondary.
Nick Moore	Long Snapper	2 years, $1.75 million	New Contract	Moore is a reliable long snapper who has been with the Ravens since 2019. He will continue to be a key part of the team's special teams unit.

Key Losses

Position	Player
Safety	Chuck Clark
Tight end	Nick Boyle
Offensive guard	Ben Powers

NFL Draft 2023

Round	Pick	Position	College	Player	NFL Fantasy Projection
1	22	WR	Boston College	Zay Flowers	120
3	86	LB	Clemson	Trenton Simpson	110
4	124	EDGE	Ole Miss	Tavius Robinson	90
5	157	CB	Stanford	Kyu Blu Kelly	80
6	199	OT	Oregon	Malaesala Aumavae-Laulu	70
7	229	S	USC	Chase Lucas	60
1	22	WR	Boston College	Zay Flowers	120

Pos	Player	Explanation
QB	Malik Willis	Willis is a dynamic quarterback with a strong arm and the ability to make plays with his feet. He could be the Ravens' future franchise quarterback.
WR	Chris Olave	Olave is a fast and athletic receiver who can stretch the field. He would be a good complement to Marquise Brown and Rashod Bateman.
OT	Trevor Penning	Penning is a physical and athletic offensive tackle who could compete for a starting job right away.
DE	David Ojabo	Ojabo is a talented pass rusher who could help to improve the Ravens' pass rush.
CB	Derek Stingley Jr.	Stingley Jr. is a former top recruit who has the potential to be a lockdown corner.

2023 SCHEDULE

PRESENTED BY Southwest

PRESEASON

#	Date	Time		Opponent	Venue	TV
1	SATURDAY, AUGUST 12	7:00 PM ET		VS EAGLES	M&T BANK STADIUM	WBAL-TV
2	MONDAY, AUGUST 21	8:00 PM ET		AT COMMANDERS	FEDEXFIELD	ESPN
3	SATURDAY, AUGUST 26	7:00 PM ET		AT BUCCANEERS	RAYMOND JAMES STADIUM	WBAL-TV

REGULAR SEASON

#	Date	Time		Opponent	Venue	TV
1	SUNDAY, SEPTEMBER 10	1:00 PM ET		VS TEXANS	M&T BANK STADIUM	CBS
2	SUNDAY, SEPTEMBER 17	1:00 PM ET		AT BENGALS	PAYCOR STADIUM	CBS
3	SUNDAY, SEPTEMBER 24	1:00 PM ET		VS COLTS	M&T BANK STADIUM	CBS
4	SUNDAY, OCTOBER 1	1:00 PM ET		AT BROWNS	CLEVELAND BROWNS STADIUM	CBS
5	SUNDAY, OCTOBER 8	1:00 PM ET*		AT STEELERS	ACRISURE STADIUM	CBS
6	SUNDAY, OCTOBER 15	9:30 AM ET		VS TITANS	TOTTENHAM HOTSPUR STADIUM	NFLN
7	SUNDAY, OCTOBER 22	1:00 PM ET*		VS LIONS	M&T BANK STADIUM	FOX
8	SUNDAY, OCTOBER 29	4:25 PM ET*		AT CARDINALS	STATE FARM STADIUM	CBS
9	SUNDAY, NOVEMBER 5	1:00 PM ET*		VS SEAHAWKS	M&T BANK STADIUM	CBS
10	SUNDAY, NOVEMBER 12	1:00 PM ET*		VS BROWNS	M&T BANK STADIUM	FOX
11	THURSDAY, NOVEMBER 16	8:15 PM ET		VS BENGALS	M&T BANK STADIUM	PRIME VIDEO
12	SUNDAY, NOVEMBER 26	8:20 PM ET*		AT CHARGERS	SOFI STADIUM	NBC
13			BYE WEEK			
14	SUNDAY, DECEMBER 10	1:00 PM ET*		VS RAMS	M&T BANK STADIUM	FOX
15	SUNDAY, DECEMBER 17	8:20 PM ET*		AT JAGUARS	TIAA BANK FIELD	NBC
16	MONDAY, DECEMBER 25	8:15 PM ET*		AT 49ERS	LEVI'S STADIUM	ABC
17	SUNDAY, DECEMBER 31	1:00 PM ET*		VS DOLPHINS	M&T BANK STADIUM	CBS
18	DATE TBD	TIME TBD		VS STEELERS	M&T BANK STADIUM	TBD

LISTEN TO THE LIVE AUDIO GAME BROADCAST ON BALTIMORERAVENS.COM, 98 ROCK, WBAL 1090 AM AND 101.5 FM.
FLEXIBLE TIME SCHEDULE - GAME TIMES AND TV NETWORKS SUBJECT TO CHANGE.

HOME AWAY

BUFFALO BILLS

A Balanced Offense Squad with a Dynamic Passing Attack

The Bills' offense is well-rounded and led by quarterback Josh Allen, known for his dynamic passing skills and running threat. His versatility makes him challenging to defend.

Solid Receivers

Stefon Diggs and Gabriel Davis anchor the receiving corps. Diggs is a big-play receiver, while Davis excels in making catches under pressure.

Strong Running Game

Devin Singletary and Zack Moss lead the ground attack. Singletary is agile and elusive, while Moss adds power in between tackles.

Team Strategy

The Bills aim to score and win through running, passing, and defense.

Strategic Play Calling

The offense capitalizes on Allen's passing strength with play-action passes and deep shots. Quick passes get playmakers in space.

Fantasy Football Picks

- Josh Allen: A must-have with his versatile passing and running skills.
- Stefon Diggs: Essential for his explosive plays.
- Gabriel Davis: Valuable for his ability to make catches under pressure.
- Devin Singletary: Useful as a pass-catching running back.
- Zack Moss: Ideal for running between tackles.

In summary, the Bills boast a balanced offense led by a skilled quarterback, strong receivers, and a capable running game. Their focus is scoring and winning games. For fantasy football, consider these players for a competitive team.

The Bills' run-pass tendencies are likely to remain the same in the 2023 season. They have a new head coach in Josh McDaniels, but he is known for his pass-happy offenses. McDaniels may even be more willing to pass the ball in 2023, especially if the Bills can improve their offensive line

Play Type	Percentage
Passing plays	56.4%
Rushing plays	43.6%

Key Additions & New Contracts

Player	Position	Contract	Key Addition	Impact on Team
Harris	Running Back	3 years, $27 million	New Contract	Harris is a proven running back who can help the Bills run the ball more effectively. He is also a good receiver out of the backfield.
Shaq Lawson	Edge Rusher	1 year, $2 million	Key Addition	Lawson is a pass rusher who can help the Bills get to the quarterback. He is also a good run defender.
Jordan Phillips	Defensive Tackle	1 year, $4 million	Key Addition	Phillips is a run stopper who can help the Bills improve their run defense. He is also a good pass rusher.
Connor McGovern	Guard	3 years, $27 million	New Contract	McGovern is a good guard who can help the Bills improve their offensive line. He is also a good run blocker.

Key Losses

Position	Player
Edge rusher	Von Miller
Linebacker	Tremaine Edmunds
Defensive end	Jerry Hughes
Running back	Devin Singletary
Wide receiver	Emmanuel Sanders

NFL Draft 2023

Round	Pick	Position	College	Player	NFL Fantasy Projection
1	25	TE	Florida	Kyle Pitts	150
2	59	WR	USC	Drake London	140
3	92	CB	Washington	Trent McDuffie	130
4	128	S	Notre Dame	Kyle Hamilton	120
5	167	EDGE	Penn State	Arnold Ebiketie	110
6	188	OT	Iowa	Tyler Linderbaum	100

Pos	Player	Reason for Selection
QB	Josh Allen	Allen is the Bills' starting quarterback and one of the best in the NFL. He is a dual-threat quarterback who can pass and run.
WR	Stefon Diggs	Diggs is the Bills' best wide receiver. He is a big-play threat who can make plays after the catch.
TE	Dawson Knox	Knox is the Bills' starting tight end. He is a good receiver and blocker.
RB	Devin Singletary	Singletary is the Bills' starting running back. He is a versatile runner who can run between the tackles and catch passes out of the backfield.
OL	Dion Dawkins	Dawkins is the Bills' starting left tackle. He is a good pass blocker and run blocker.

■ HOME ■ AWAY

PRESEASON				
WIVB 4	08/12	PS01 vs 1:00 PM ET	IND	
WIVB 4	08/19	PS02 AT 6:30 PM ET	PIT	
WIVB 4	08/26	PS03 AT 1:00 PM ET	CHI	
	09/11	WK01 8:15 PM ET	NYJ	
NFL	09/17	WK02 vs 1:00 PM ET	LV	
NFL	09/24	WK03 AT 1:00 PM ET	WSH	
NFL	10/01	WK04 vs 1:00 PM ET	MIA	

LONDON	10/08	WK05 9:30 AM ET	JAX*	
SUNDAY NIGHT FOOTBALL	10/15	WK06 vs 8:20 PM ET	NYG	
NFL	10/22	WK07 AT 1:00 PM ET	NE	
THURSDAY NIGHT FOOTBALL	10/26	WK08 vs 8:15 PM ET	TB	
SUNDAY NIGHT FOOTBALL	11/05	WK09 AT 8:20 PM ET	CIN	
ESPN MONDAY NIGHT FOOTBALL	11/13	WK10 vs 8:15 PM ET	DEN	
NFL	11/19	WK11 vs 4:25 PM ET	NYJ	

NFL	11/26	WK12 AT 4:25 PM ET	PHI	
	WK13	— BYE WK —		
NFL	12/10	WK14 AT 4:25 PM ET	KC	
FOX NFL	12/17	WK15 vs 4:25 PM ET	DAL	
peacock	12/23	WK16 AT 8:00 PM ET	LAC	
NFL	12/31	WK17 vs 1:00 PM ET	NE	
	TBD	WK18 AT TBD	MIA	

*Tottenham Hotspur Stadium in London | All Dates & Times Subject to Change

BUFFALO BILLS 2023 SCHEDULE

PRESENTED BY aloft AT 510

— FOR TICKETS

 VISIT BUFFALOBILLS.COM/TICKETS

 CALL 1-877-BB-TICKS (1-877-228-4257)

 EMAIL TICKETSALES@BILLS.NFL.NET

22

Meet the Panthers

A team that loves to run the ball first, led by their young and skilled quarterback, Sam Darnold. He's not only a great passer but also a running threat, giving defenses a tough time.

Christian McCaffrey, a star running back, makes opponents nervous every time he gets the ball. He's one of the best in the league.

While their passing game isn't as strong as their running, it's still decent. D.J. Moore is a big-play receiver, while Robbie Anderson shines in tight situations.

The Panthers focus on controlling the game clock and keeping rivals' offenses off the field. They do this by running the ball well and playing solid defense.

Their tactics make the most of McCaffrey's running skills — using zone runs and quick passes. They aim to get him into open space.

In short, the Panthers rely on running, backed by a promising young quarterback. They have solid running backs and a decent passing game. Their goal? Control the game and win.

For your NFL fantasy team, consider:
- Sam Darnold: A quarterback with potential and surrounded by strong players.
- Christian McCaffrey: A must-have running back.
- D.J. Moore: A receiver who can challenge defenses deep.
- Robbie Anderson: A receiver who shines in tight spots.

Play Type	Percentage
Passing plays	49.4%
Rushing plays	50.6%

The Panthers' 2022 game plan:
1. Run-Centric: They favored running plays (50.6%) over passing (45.4% league avg.).
2. Balanced Passing: Managed 234.2 passing yds/game and 187.1 rushing yds/game.
3. McCaffrey's Impact: Strong RB core led by Christian McCaffrey influenced their run-first style.
4. Solid Line: Their offensive line allowed 29 sacks (11th fewest) — key for successful rushes.
5. Developing QB: Sam Darnold's skills evolving, better passer than runner.
6. 2023 Outlook: New coach Ben McAdoo leans to run-heavy approach; health could elevate running focus.

Key Additions & New Contracts

Player	Position	Contract	Key Addition	Impact on Team
Baker Mayfield	Quarterback	4 years, $135 million	New Contract	Mayfield is a veteran quarterback who can provide stability at the position. He is expected to be the starter in 2023.
Rashad Penny	Running Back	3 years, $10 million	New Contract	Penny is a talented running back who can provide a boost to the Panthers' rushing attack. He is expected to be the starter in 2023.
DJ Moore	Wide Receiver	4 years, $85 million	New Contract	Moore is a star wide receiver who is one of the best in the NFL. He is expected to continue to be a key playmaker for the Panthers' offense.

Key Losses

Position	Player
Edge rusher	Haason Reddick
Wide receiver	D.J. Moore
Tight end	Ian Thomas
Offensive tackle	Taylor Moton
Linebacker	Shaq Thompson

NFL Draft 2023

Round	Pick	Position	College	Player	NFL Fantasy Projection
1	6	OT	Mississippi	Charles Cross	120
2	42	WR	Ohio State	Chris Olave	110
3	74	CB	Clemson	Andrew Booth Jr.	90
4	106	RB	Georgia	Zamir White	100
5	169	EDGE	Penn State	Arnold Ebiketie	80
6	191	WR	Alabama	John Metchie III	70
6	214	TE	USC	Michael Trigg	60

Pos	Player	Why chosen
QB	Matt Corral	The Panthers need a young quarterback to develop behind Sam Darnold. Corral is a talented passer who has the potential to be a star.
WR	Chris Olave	The Panthers need a wide receiver who can stretch the field. Olave is a fast and athletic receiver who can make plays after the catch.
DE	David Ojabo	The Panthers need an edge rusher to help their pass rush. Ojabo is a talented pass rusher who has the potential to be a difference-maker.
CB	Trent McDuffie	The Panthers need a cornerback to solidify their secondary. McDuffie is a good cover corner who can play both man and zone coverage.
OT	Trevor Penning	The Panthers need an offensive tackle to protect their quarterback. Penning is a big and physical tackle who can play both left and right tackle.

2023 SCHEDULE

PS1	AUG 12	4:00PM	Jets
PS2	AUG 18	7:00PM	Giants
PS3	AUG 25	8:00PM	Lions

WEEK	Date	Time	Opponent
1	SEP 10	1:00PM	Falcons
2	SEP 18	7:15PM	Saints
3	SEP 24	4:05PM	Seahawks
4	OCT 1	1:00PM	Vikings
5	OCT 8	1:00PM	Lions
6	OCT 15	1:00PM	Dolphins
7	BYE		
8	OCT 29	1:00PM	Texans
9	NOV 5	4:05PM	Colts
10	NOV 9	8:15PM	Bears
11	NOV 19	1:00PM	Cowboys
12	NOV 26	1:00PM	Titans
13	DEC 3	1:00PM	Buccaneers
14	DEC 10	1:00PM	Saints
15	TBD		Falcons
16	DEC 24	1:00PM	Packers
17	DEC 31	1:00PM	Jaguars
18	TBD		Buccaneers

HOME

AWAY

DATES & TIMES (ET) SUBJECT TO CHANGE

PURCHASE TICKETS AT PANTHERS.COM/TICKETS

CHICAGO BEARS

A Work in Progress with a Young and Unproven Quarterback

Let's break it down for NFL enthusiasts:

1. Bears' Progress with Justin Fields: The Bears are evolving under young quarterback Justin Fields. He's got potential but is still learning the ropes. Fields is a good passer, improving his decision-making under pressure.

2. Strong Running Game: David Montgomery leads a solid running backs crew. He's great at running between the tackles and catching passes.

3. Balanced Passing Game: The passing game is decent, with Darnell Mooney and Byron Pringle as key receivers. Mooney's speed is a threat, while Pringle excels at holding onto the ball.

4. Building Around Fields: The team's focus is nurturing Fields into a star. They emphasize running the ball and strong defense to support his growth.

5. Tailoring Schemes to Fields: The Bears tailor their plays to Fields' mobility. Expect play-action passes and rollouts, plus quick passes to their playmakers.

6. Evolving Team: The Bears are a work in progress with promising players. They strive to get better and rack up wins.

For Fantasy Football:

1. Justin Fields: A promising QB with potential and surrounded by good teammates. Worth a look if you want an improving quarterback.

2. David Montgomery: A running back who can catch passes. A solid choice for fantasy teams in need of versatile backs.

3. Darnell Mooney: A receiver who can stretch defenses. Good pick if you want a player who can break free for big plays.

4. Byron Pringle: Reliable in traffic, Pringle is a solid receiver pick for those seeking someone who can make plays in tight spots.

Play Type	Percentage
Passing plays	48.8%
Rushing plays	51.2%

The Bears' run-pass tendencies are likely to remain the same in the 2023 season. They have a new head coach in Matt Eberflus, but he is known for his run-heavy offenses. Eberflus may even be more willing to run the ball in 2023, especially if the Bears can stay healthy.

26

Key Additions & New Contracts

Player	Position	Contract	Key Addition	Impact on Team
PJ Walker	Quarterback	2 years, $11 million	Key Addition	Walker is a young and talented quarterback who could compete with Justin Fields for the starting job.
Tre'Vius Slay	Cornerback	3 years, $54 million	Key Addition	Slay is a proven veteran cornerback who will help improve the Bears' secondary.
D'Onta Foreman	Running Back	2 years, $10 million	New Contract	Foreman is a bruising running back who can help the Bears run the ball more effectively.
Robert Tonyan	Tight End	1 year, $3.5 million	New Contract	Tonyan is a big-play tight end who can help the Bears' passing game.
Andrew Billings	Defensive Tackle	1 year, $3.5 million	New Contract	Billings is a strong run-stuffer who can help the Bears' defense stop the run.

Key Losses

Position	Player
Edge rusher	Khalil Mack
Cornerback	Jaylon Johnson
Wide receiver	Allen Robinson II
Offensive tackle	Larry Borom
Guard	James Daniels

NFL Draft 2023

Round	Pick	Position	College	Player	Fantasy Projection
1	10	OT	Tennessee	Darnell Wright	100
2	53	DT	Florida	Gervon Dexter	80
3	64	CB	Miami (FL)	Tyrique Stevenson	70
4	115	WR	USC	Drake London	60
5	148	RB	Texas A&M	Isaiah Spiller	50
6	181	OT	Central Michigan	Bernhard Raimann	40

Position	Player	Explanation
QB	Justin Fields	The Bears' first-round pick in 2021, Fields is still developing but has shown flashes of potential.
RB	David Montgomery	A solid running back who can be a reliable option in the Bears' offense.
WR	Darnell Mooney	A speedy receiver who can make plays downfield.
TE	Cole Kmet	A young tight end who has the potential to be a major weapon in the Bears' offense.
OT	Teven Jenkins	A first-round pick in 2022, Jenkins is still learning the ropes but has the potential to be a franchise left tackle.

2023
BEARS
SEASON SCHEDULE

Preseason

SAT, AUG 12	TITANS	NOON	FOX
Sat, Aug 19	at Indianapolis	6:00pm	FOX
SAT, AUG 26	BILLS	NOON	FOX

Regular Season

SUN, SEP 10	PACKERS	3:25PM	FOX
Sun, Sep 17	at Tampa Bay	Noon	FOX
Sun, Sep 24	at Kansas City	3:25pm	FOX
SUN, OCT 1	BRONCOS	NOON	CBS
Thu, Oct 5	at Washington	7:15pm	PRIME*
SUN, OCT 15	VIKINGS	NOON	FOX*
SUN, OCT 22	RAIDERS	NOON	FOX*
Sun, Oct 29	at LA Chargers	7:20pm	NBC*
Sun, Nov 5	at New Orleans	NOON	CBS*
THU, NOV 9	PANTHERS	7:15PM	PRIME*
Sun, Nov 19	at Detroit	Noon	FOX*
Mon, Nov 27	at Minnesota	7:15pm	ESPN+
	Bye Week		
SUN, DEC 10	LIONS	NOON	FOX+
TBD	at Cleveland	TBD	TBD+
SUN, DEC 24	CARDINALS	3:25PM	FOX+
SUN, DEC 31	FALCONS	NOON	CBS+
TBD	at Green Bay	TBD	TBD+

BEARS

*Game time subject to change beginning Week 5
+Game date and time subject to change beginning Week 12
All games Central Time

CINCINNATI BENGALS

A Young and Explosive Offense with a Prolific Passing Attack

The Bengals boast a young, energetic offense led by quarterback Joe Burrow, who's in his second year. He's both a skilled passer and a mobile threat. Their receiving squad, helmed by Ja'Marr Chase and Tee Higgins, shines. Chase is a big-play receiver while Higgins excels in crowded spaces.

Cincinnati's strategy centers on scoring and victory, utilizing passing and solid defense. Their offense is built around Burrow's arm, using play-action passes and deep throws. Quick passes are also employed to exploit their playmakers' abilities.

In fantasy football, consider these players:
- Joe Burrow: A vital addition with potential, backed by talented receivers.
- Ja'Marr Chase: A top-tier receiver who poses a scoring threat each time he handles the ball.
- Tee Higgins: A suitable choice for those seeking a receiver adept at making plays in tight situations.

Play Type	Percentage
Passing plays	63.3%
Rushing plays	36.7%

The Bengals in 2022 leaned heavily towards passing plays, using them in 63.3% of their offensive plays, higher than the league average of 55.2%. While their running game was decent, it wasn't as strong as their passing game. They averaged 143.3 rushing yards and 273.8 passing yards per game.

Here's why they favored passing in 2022:

1. They boast a talented receiving duo: Ja'Marr Chase and Tee Higgins, among the best in the NFL.
2. Their quarterback, Joe Burrow, is skilled at passing.
3. Their offensive line is solid, allowing just 29 sacks (11th fewest) in 2022.

Expect their pass-heavy approach to continue in 2023, even under new head coach Zac Taylor, known for favoring passing offenses. Taylor might emphasize passing even more this year, especially if the team remains injury-free.

Key Additions & New Contracts

Player	Position	Contract	Key Addition	Impact on Team
Hayden Hurst	Tight end	3 years, $27 million	Key addition	Hurst is a good receiving tight end who can help the Bengals' offense. He had 56 catches for 571 yards and 6 touchdowns in 2022.
Nick Scott	Safety	3 years, $10.5 million	New contract	Scott is a good safety who can help the Bengals' defense. He had 65 tackles and 2 interceptions in 2022.
Germaine Pratt	Linebacker	4 years, $46.6 million	New contract	Pratt is a good linebacker who can help the Bengals' defense. He had 104 tackles and 2 sacks in 2022.
Ted Karras	Center	3 years, $18 million	Re-signed	Karras is a good center who can help the Bengals' offense. He was a key part of the Bengals' offensive line that helped Joe Burrow win the NFL MVP award in 2022.

Key Losses

Position	Player
Cornerback	Eli Apple
Defensive end	Trey Hendrickson
Linebacker	Logan Wilson
Wide receiver	Tee Higgins

NFL Draft 2023

Round	Pick	Position	College	Player	Fantasy Projection
1	28	Edge	Georgia	Nolan Smith	120
2	60	WR	USC	Drake London	110
3	95	DT	Georgia	Devonte Wyatt	90
4	131	CB	Cincinnati	Sauce Gardner	100
5	174	OG	Kentucky	Darian Kinnard	80
6	217	OT	Central Michigan	Bernhard Raimann	70

Pos	Player	Why chosen
QB	Joe Burrow	Burrow is the franchise quarterback and the team's most important player.
WR	Ja'Marr Chase	Chase is a superstar wide receiver and one of the best in the NFL.
LT	Jonah Williams	Williams is a good left tackle and he has the potential to be a franchise player.
DE	Trey Hendrickson	Hendrickson is a good pass rusher and he has the potential to be a difference-maker in the Bengals' defense.
DT	D.J. Reader	Reader is a good run defender and he helps to clog up the middle of the Bengals' defense.
CB	Sauce Gardner	Gardner is a good cover corner and he has the potential to be a starter in the Bengals' secondary.

2023 SCHEDULE

2023 PRESEASON

1	FRI	AUG 11	GREEN BAY	7:00 PM
2	FRI	AUG 18	@ ATLANTA	7:30 PM
3	SAT	AUG 26	@ WASHINGTON	6:05 PM

2023 REGULAR SEASON

1	SUN	SEP 10	@ CLEVELAND	1:00 PM
2	SUN	SEP 17	BALTIMORE	1:00 PM
3	MON	SEP 25	LA RAMS*	8:15 PM
4	SUN	OCT 1	@ TENNESSEE	1:00 PM
5	SUN	OCT 8	@ ARIZONA	4:05 PM
6	SUN	OCT 15	SEATTLE	1:00 PM
7	----	-------	BYE WEEK	-------
8	SUN	OCT 29	@ SAN FRANCISCO	4:25 PM
9	SUN	NOV 5	BUFFALO*	8:20 PM
10	SUN	NOV 12	HOUSTON	1:00 PM
11	THURS	NOV 16	@ BALTIMORE*	8:15 PM
12	SUN	NOV 26	PITTSBURGH	1:00 PM
13	MON	DEC 4	@ JACKSONVILLE*	8:15 PM
14	SUN	DEC 10	INDIANAPOLIS	1:00 PM
15	TBD	DEC 16/17	MINNESOTA	TBD
16	SAT	DEC 23	@ PITTSBURGH	4:30 PM
17	SUN	DEC 31	@ KANSAS CITY	4:25 PM
18	TBD	JAN 6/7	CLEVELAND	TBD

ALL TIMES EASTERN | DATES & TIMES SUBJECT TO CHANGE | *INDICATES PRIMETIME GAME

BENGALS.COM/TICKETS
513.621.8383

RULE THE JUNGLE

CLEVELAND BROWNS

Dynamic Offense Led by Deshaun Watson's Versatility

In the realm of the Cleveland Browns, a dynamic and well-rounded offense emerges as a force to be reckoned with. Anchored by quarterback Deshaun Watson, this team showcases a distinctive passing prowess along with a knack for ground game domination.

1. Versatile Quarterback: Deshaun Watson spearheads the Browns' offensive charge, not just with his precise passing but also with his ability to rush. This dual-threat dynamism makes Watson a formidable challenge for opposing defenses.

2. Receiving Arsenal:The Browns boast a solid group of receivers, with Amari Cooper and Donovan Peoples-Jones leading the charge. Cooper's penchant for explosive plays stretches defenses thin, while Peoples-Jones excels in clutch situations.

3. Ground Game Excellence: The Browns' ground attack is a force to be reckoned with, thanks to Nick Chubb and Kareem Hunt. Chubb's power running and Hunt's elusiveness add diversity and complexity to their offensive strategy.

4. Winning Philosophy: The Browns' primary goal is to rack up points and secure victories. Their approach involves a balanced mix of running, passing, and solid defensive plays.

5. Strategic Offense: Cleveland's offensive schemes align with Watson's skill set, making the most of his adept passing. They employ play-action and deep shots to exploit his strengths, often using quick passes to deliver the ball to their playmakers in open spaces.

For Your Fantasy Football Lineup:

1. Deshaun Watson: An essential addition to any fantasy lineup, Watson's versatility as a passer and runner makes him a standout choice, backed by talented teammates.
2. Amari Cooper: Ideal for those seeking a receiver capable of creating explosive plays, Cooper is your go-to option.
3. Donovan Peoples-Jones: A wise pick if you're after a receiver who thrives amidst traffic and delivers in crucial moments.
4. Nick Chubb: For a reliable running back capable of pounding through defenses, Chubb is the name to keep in mind.
5. Kareem Hunt: If you're in search of a running back who excels in open spaces, Hunt is a valuable asset for your fantasy football team.

Cleveland Browns' run-pass tendencies in the 2022 NFL season

Play Type	Percentage
Passing plays	57.3%
Rushing plays	42.7%

32

Key Additions & New Contracts

Player	Position	Contract	Key Addition	Impact on Team
Deion Jones	LB	3 years, $52.5 million	Key Addition	Jones is a three-time Pro Bowler who will add much-needed experience and leadership to the Browns' defense.
Jadeveon Clowney	DE	1 year, $10 million	Key Addition	Clowney is a former All-Pro who will provide the Browns with a pass-rushing boost.
Mack Wilson	LB	3 years, $22.5 million	New Contract	Wilson is a young, versatile linebacker who will be a key part of the Browns' defense for years to come.
Donovan Peoples-Jones	WR	3 years, $24 million	New Contract	Peoples-Jones is a developing receiver who has shown flashes of potential. He will be looking to build on his 2022 season in 2023.

Key Losses

Position	Player
Defensive tackle	Dalvin Tomlinson
Edge rusher	Jadeveon Clowney
Center	Ethan Pocic

NFL Draft 2023

Round	Pick	Position	College	Player	Fantasy Projection
1	13	WR	Tennessee	Cedric Tillman	70
3	74	DT	Baylor	Siaki Ika	60
4	111	OT	Ohio State	Dawand Jones	50
5	140	CB	Northwestern	Cameron Mitchell	40
6	176	RB	Texas A&M	Isaiah Spiller	30
7	228	OG	Iowa	Tyler Linderbaum	20
7	252	EDGE	Penn State	Arnold Ebiketie	10

os	Player	Why chosen
QB	C.J. Stroud	He is the consensus top quarterback in the 2023 NFL Draft and has the potential to be a franchise quarterback.
WR	Jameson Williams	He is a big-play receiver who could be a threat to score every time he touches the ball.
OT	Charles Cross	He is a good pass blocker and he has the potential to be a franchise left tackle.
EDGE	Aidan Hutchinson	He is a good pass rusher and he has the potential to be a difference-maker in the Browns' defense.
LB	Nakobe Dean	He is a good coverage linebacker and he has the potential to be a starter in the Browns' defense.

BROWNS
2023 SEASON SCHEDULE

HOME AWAY

AUGUST

HOF | **AUG 3** 8:00PM / NEUTRAL

PRE 1 | **AUG 11** 7:30PM / HOME

PRE 2 | **AUG 17** 7:30PM / AWAY

PRE 3 | **AUG 26** 1:00PM / AWAY

SEPTEMBER

WK 1 | **SEP 10** 1:00PM / HOME

MNF

WK 2 | **SEP 18** 8:15PM / AWAY

WK 3 | **SEP 24** 1:00PM / HOME

FOR TICKETS: 440.891.5050 OR CLEVELANDBROWNS.COM

OCTOBER

WK 4 | **OCT 1** 1:00PM / HOME

WK 5 | **BYE**

WK 6 | **OCT 15** 1:00PM / HOME

WK 7 | **OCT 22** 1:00PM / AWAY

WK 8 | **OCT 29** 4:05PM / AWAY

NOVEMBER

WK 9 | **NOV 5** 1:00PM / HOME

WK 10 | **NOV 12** 1:00PM / AWAY

WK 11 | **NOV 19** 1:00PM / HOME

WK 12 | **NOV 26** 4:05PM / AWAY

DECEMBER

WK 13 | **DEC 3** 4:25PM / AWAY

WK 14 | **DEC 10** 1:00PM / HOME

WK 15 | **TBD** HOME

WK 16 | **DEC 24** 1:00PM / AWAY

TNF

WK 17 | **DEC 28** 8:15PM / HOME

JANUARY

WK 18 | **TBD** AWAY

FOLLOW US

 /CLEVELANDBROWNS /BROWNS

@CLEVELANDBROWNS @BROWNS

@BROWNS

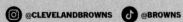

Unveiling the Dallas Cowboys' Explosive Passing Arsenal

Quarterback Dak Prescott:Fantasy Essential
- Prescott's dynamic arm and mobility are crucial for your fantasy roster.

Wide Receivers CeeDee Lamb and Amari Cooper:
- Lamb: Explosive playmaker, perfect for big gains.
- Cooper: Reliable in tight situations, a traffic specialist.

Running Back Ezekiel Elliott:
- Powerful runner, though recent effectiveness varies.

Cowboys' Strategy: Passing Prowess
- Emphasize passing, exploiting Prescott's arm strength.

Strategies:
- Quick passes, using playmakers in open space.
- Prescott's play-action and deep throws as weapons.

Fantasy Picks:
- Prescott: Must-have passer and playmaker.
- Lamb: Explosive option for game-changing plays.
- Cooper: Ideal for navigating tight defensive coverage.
- Elliott: Strong between tackles, albeit with fluctuations.

In a Nutshell:
The Cowboys revolve around Prescott's arm, employing quick throws and savvy play-action. Prescott, Lamb, Cooper, and Elliott offer diverse fantasy options for points and victories.

Play Type	Percentage
Passing plays	62.9%
Rushing plays	37.1%

Passing Power: The Cowboys favored the air, calling passes on 62.9% of snaps (above 55.2% league average). Their passing game thrived, netting 258.2 yards per game. A respectable ground game added 136 rushing yards.
Air Arsenal:
  1. Dynamic Duo: Receivers CeeDee Lamb and Amari Cooper shone.
  2. Prescott's Precision: QB Dak Prescott's arm strength fueled the passes.
  3. Strong Shield: Only 33 sacks allowed by their offensive line.
2023 Outlook: New coach Mike McCarthy's pass-heavy approach is set to continue. His history signals even more air time, boosted by player health. The Cowboys' skies remain vibrant.

Key Additions & New Contracts

Player	Position	Contract	Key Addition/New Contract	Impact on Team
Keanu Neal	Linebacker	4 years, $40 million	Key Addition	Neal is a versatile linebacker who can play multiple positions. He will help to improve the Cowboys' run defense.
Randy Gregory	Defensive End	5 years, $70 million	Key Addition	Gregory is a pass-rusher who can get to the quarterback. He will help to improve the Cowboys' pass rush.
Tyler Smith	Offensive Tackle	4 years, $54.4 million	New Contract	Smith is a talented offensive tackle who can protect Dak Prescott. He will help to improve the Cowboys' offensive line.
James Washington	Wide Receiver	3 years, $10.5 million	New Contract	Washington is a deep threat who can stretch the field. He will help to improve the Cowboys' passing game.

Key Losses

Position	Player
Offensive Tackle	Tyron Smith
Defensive End	Randy Gregory
Tight End	Dalton Schultz
Wide Receiver	Michael Gallup
Cornerback	Jourdan Lewis

NFL Draft 2023

Round	Pick	Position	College	Player	NFL Fantasy Projection
1	25	OT	Mississippi	Charles Cross	90
2	56	WR	USC	Drake London	90
3	88	LB	Georgia	Nakobe Dean	80
4	129	CB	Washington	Kyler Gordon	70
5	160	DT	Florida	Gervon Dexter	60
6	181	S	TCU	Bryan Cook	50
6	212	TE	Coastal Carolina	Isaiah Likely	40

Pos	Player	Why chosen
QB	Sam Howell	Howell is a dual-threat quarterback who has the potential to be a franchise quarterback. He is a good passer and he can also run the ball.
WR	George Pickens	Pickens is a big-play receiver who can stretch the field. He is a good route runner and he has good hands.
OT	Bernhard Raimann	Raimann is a good pass blocker and he has the potential to be a starter at left tackle. He is a tall and athletic player who is still developing.
EDGE	David Ojabo	Ojabo is a good pass rusher who has the potential to be a difference-maker in the Cowboys' defense. He is a fast and explosive player who can get to the quarterback.

2023 SCHEDULE

Date	Preseason (TV)	Central Time
SAT, AUG. 12	**JACKSONVILLE JAGUARS (CBS 11)**	**4:00 PM**
Sat, Aug. 19	@ Seattle Seahawks (CBS 11)	9:00 pm
SAT, AUG. 26	**LAS VEGAS RAIDERS (CBS 11)**	**7:00 PM**

Date	Regular Season (TV)	Central Time
Sun, Sept. 10	@ New York Giants (NBC)	7:20 pm
SUN, SEPT. 17	**NEW YORK JETS (CBS)**	**3:25 PM**
Sun, Sept. 24	@ Arizona Cardinals (FOX)	3:25 pm
SUN, OCT. 1	**NEW ENGLAND PATRIOTS (FOX)**	**3:25 PM**
Sun, Oct. 8	@ San Francisco 49ers (NBC)	7:20 pm
Mon, Oct. 16	@ Los Angeles Chargers (ESPN)	7:15 pm
	BYE	
SUN, OCT. 29	**LOS ANGELES RAMS (FOX)**	**12:00 PM**
Sun, Nov. 5	@ Philadelphia Eagles (FOX)	3:25 pm
SUN, NOV. 12	**NEW YORK GIANTS (FOX)**	**3:25 PM**
Sun, Nov. 19	@ Carolina Panthers (FOX)	12:00 pm
THUR, NOV. 23	**WASHINGTON COMMANDERS (CBS)**	**3:30 PM**
THUR, NOV. 30	**SEATTLE SEAHAWKS (PRIME)**	**7:15 PM**
SUN, DEC. 10	**PHILADELPHIA EAGLES (NBC)**	**7:20 PM**
Sun, Dec. 17	@ Buffalo Bills (FOX)	3:25 pm
Sun, Dec. 24	@ Miami Dolphins (FOX)	3:25 PM
SAT, DEC. 30	**DETROIT LIONS (ESPN/ABC)**	**7:15 PM**
Sat/Sun, Jan. 6/7	@ Washington Commanders (TBD)	TBD

Home games in **BOLD.** Game times and television broadcasts are subject to change.

All Dallas Cowboys games can be heard locally in English (105.3 FM The Fan)
and Spanish (La Grande 107.5 FM) and across the southwest on the Dallas Cowboys Radio Network.

DENVER BRONCOS

A Ground-Pounding Offense and the Emergence of a Young Quarterback

1. Running the Show:
Broncos prioritize ground game, with QB Russell Wilson's dual threat causing headaches for defenses.

2. Running Back Power:
Javonte Williams adds muscle between tackles and catches passes smartly.

3. Balanced Passing:
Courtland Sutton's explosive plays and Jerry Jeudy's precise receptions shine.

4. Clock Masters and Defense:
Broncos manage time, rely on robust defense to control rival offenses.

5. Offensive Approach:
Wilson's agility sparks zone runs, play-action passes, and quick throws.

Fantasy Picks:
- Russell Wilson: Potential-packed QB.
- Javonte Williams: Tough runner.
- Courtland Sutton: Big-play receiver.
- Jerry Jeudy: Traffic maestro.

Broncos blend ground game with a budding QB, poised to carve their niche.

Play Type	Percentage
Passing plays	49.4%
Rushing plays	50.6%

In 2022, the Broncos leaned heavily on their running game, running the ball on over half of their plays (50.6%). This was a bit more than the league average (45.4%). While their passing game wasn't as dominant, it still held its ground, with 224.1 passing yards per game and 187.6 rushing yards per game.

Run-First Reasons:
1. Strong Running Backs: With Javonte Williams in their roster, they boast one of the NFL's top running backs.
2. Sturdy Offensive Line: Their O-line allowed just 28 sacks, ranked 16th lowest in the league.
3. Developing QB: Russell Wilson, their quarterback, is learning the offense, which means they leaned on the run more.

2023 Outlook:
Expect a familiar theme in 2023. New head coach Nathaniel Hackett has a history of favoring the run. With his penchant for run-heavy strategies, there's a chance the Broncos will hit the ground even more. If their roster remains healthy, prepare for another year of ground gains and gridiron action.

Key Additions & New Contracts

Player	Position	Contract	Key Addition/New Contract	Impact on Team
Russell Wilson	Quarterback	3 years, $150 million	Key Addition	Wilson is a proven quarterback who can lead the Broncos to the playoffs.
Randy Gregory	Defensive End	5 years, $70 million	Key Addition	Gregory is a pass rusher who can help the Broncos' defense get more sacks.
D.J. Jones	Defensive Tackle	3 years, $54 million	Key Addition	Jones is a run stopper who can help the Broncos' defense get better against the run.
Bradley Chubb	Defensive End	5 years, $105 million	New Contract	Chubb is a pass rusher who is coming off a major injury. He will be looking to bounce back in 2023.
Tim Patrick	Wide Receiver	3 years, $34.5 million	New Contract	Patrick is a good receiver who can help the Broncos' offense.

Key Losses

Position	Player
Offensive Tackle	Garett Bolles
Defensive End	D.J. Jones
Linebacker	Josey Jewell
Cornerback	Kyle Fuller
Safety	Kareem Jackson

NFL Draft 2023

Round	Pick	Position	College	Player	Fantasy Projection
1	28	CB	Washington	Trent McDuffie	100
3	96	WR	USC	Drake London	90
4	118	OT	Tennessee	Nicholas Petit-Frere	80
5	146	EDGE	Kentucky	Josh Paschal	70
6	174	S	TCU	Trevon Moehrig	60
7	233	RB	Baylor	Abram Smith	50
1	28	CB	Washington	Trent McDuffie	100

Pos	Player	Explanation
QB	Drew Lock	Lock is the incumbent starter and has shown flashes of potential. He could be a good value pick in the later rounds of the draft.
RB	Javonte Williams	Williams is a rising star and is one of the best running backs in the NFL. He is a must-have for any fantasy football team.
WR	Jerry Jeudy	Jeudy is a talented wide receiver who has been hampered by injuries in his first two seasons. He is a buy-low candidate in fantasy football.
TE	Albert Okwuegbunam	Okwuegbunam is a athletic tight end who has the potential to be a big-play threat. He is a sleeper pick in fantasy football.

2023 FOOTBALL
SCHEDULE

PRESEASON

HOME · AWAY

1	FRI, AUG. 11	@ Arizona	State Farm Stadium	7 p.m. MST	9.
2	SAT, AUG. 19	@ San Francisco	Levi's Stadium	5:30 p.m. PT	9.
3	SAT, AUG. 26	L.A. RAMS	Empower Field at Mile High	7 p.m. MT	9.

REGULAR SEASON

1	SUN, SEPT. 10	LAS VEGAS	Empower Field at Mile High	2:25 p.m. MT	◉
2	SUN, SEPT. 17	WASHINGTON	Empower Field at Mile High	2:25 p.m. MT	◉
3	SUN, SEPT. 24	@ Miami	Hard Rock Stadium	1 p.m. ET	◉
4	SUN, OCT. 1	@ Chicago	Soldier Field	12 p.m. CT	◉
5	SUN, OCT. 8	N.Y. JETS	Empower Field at Mile High	2:25 p.m. MT	◉ *
6	THU, OCT. 12	@ Kansas City	GEHA Field at Arrowhead Stadium	7:15 p.m. CT	prime video
7	SUN, OCT. 22	GREEN BAY	Empower Field at Mile High	2:25 p.m. MT	◉ *
8	SUN, OCT. 29	KANSAS CITY	Empower Field at Mile High	2:25 p.m. MT	◉ *

WEEK 9 BYE

10	MON, NOV. 13	@ Buffalo	Highmark Stadium	8:15 p.m. ET	ESPN
11	SUN, NOV. 19	MINNESOTA	Empower Field at Mile High	6:20 p.m. MT	NBC *
12	SUN, NOV. 26	CLEVELAND	Empower Field at Mile High	2:05 p.m. MT	FOX *
13	SUN, DEC. 3	@ Houston	NRG Stadium	3:05 p.m. CT	◉ *
14	SUN, DEC. 10	@ L.A. Chargers	SoFi Stadium	1:25 p.m. PT	◉ *
15	SAT/SUN, DEC. 16/17	@ Detroit	Ford Field	TBD	TBD *
16	SUN, DEC. 24	NEW ENGLAND	Empower Field at Mile High	6:15 p.m. MT	NFL NETWORK *
17	SUN, DEC. 31	L.A. CHARGERS	Empower Field at Mile High	2:25 p.m. MT	◉ *
18	SAT/SUN, JAN. 6/7	@ Las Vegas	Allegiant Stadium	TBD	TBD *

Unveiling the Detroit Lions' Emerging Offensive Powerhouse Led by Young Star Quarterback

The Detroit Lions are a team in transition, guided by quarterback Jared Goff. While Goff has impressive passing skills, he's still adapting to the offense and building his comfort in passing situations.

An exciting receiver lineup is led by Amon-Ra St. Brown, who's known for game-changing plays that stretch defenses. Additionally, St. Brown's agility allows him to shine as a possession receiver amidst tight coverage.

Fueling the Lions' attack is the formidable running game orchestrated by D'Andre Swift. Swift's prowess in both power running and pass-catching makes him a versatile asset.

The Lions are committed to nurturing Goff's growth while crafting a winning squad. They accomplish this through balanced playcalling, mixing runs, passes, and staunch defense.

Their offensive strategies harness Goff's throwing talents. Expect frequent play-action passes and deep shots to exploit open spaces. Quick, precise passes also play a role, delivering the ball to key playmakers with room to maneuver.

In essence, the Lions are a blossoming offense steered by an emerging, skilled quarterback. They're an ever-evolving team dedicated to both progress and triumph.

Fantasy Football Prospects:

1. Jared Goff: A prime pick for fantasy football managers seeking an upward trajectory in their quarterback. With glimpses of excellence and a strong supporting receiver corps, Goff holds potential.
2. Amon-Ra St. Brown: A fantastic choice for those craving a receiver capable of challenging defenses deep.
3. D'Andre Swift: An excellent selection for fantasy managers on the hunt for a versatile running back skilled in both power running and catching passes.

Play Type	Percentage
Passing plays	56.3%
Rushing plays	43.7%

Why the Focus on Passing?

- Solid Receivers: Amon-Ra St. Brown, D'Andre Swift formed a strong duo.
- Skilled Quarterback: Jared Goff's accurate passing played a role.
- Strong Protection: Just 32 sacks allowed, ranking 12th lowest.

Future Outlook: New coach Dan Campbell's pass-friendly style will likely continue in 2023. Expect Lions to maintain a balanced yet pass-focused approach, possibly amping up the aerial game.

Key Additions & New Contracts

Player	Position	Contract	Key Addition/New Contract	Impact on Team
David Montgomery	Running Back	3 years, $33 million	New Contract	Montgomery is a talented running back who can help the Lions run the ball more effectively.
Cameron Sutton	Cornerback	3 years, $48 million	Key Addition	Sutton is a good cornerback who can help the Lions improve their secondary.
Emmanuel Moseley	Cornerback	1 year, $4 million	New Contract	Moseley is a good cornerback who can help the Lions depth at the position.
Will Harris	Safety	1 year, $2.53 million, fully guaranteed	New Contract	Harris is a versatile safety who can play multiple positions. He will help the Lions depth at the position.
C.J. Moore	Safety	2 years, $4.5 million	New Contract	Moore is a good safety who can help the Lions improve their secondary.
Graham Glasgow	Guard	1 year, $1.3 million	New Contract	Glasgow is a veteran guard who can help the Lions improve their offensive line.

Key Losses

Position	Player
Running back	D'Andre Swift
Edge rusher	Romeo Okwara
Defensive tackle	Michael Brockers
Linebacker	Jamie Collins
Safety	Tracy Walker

NFL Draft 2023

Round	Pick	Position	College	Player	NFL Fantasy Projection
1	2	EDGE	Oregon	Kayvon Thibodeaux	90
2	34	WR	Alabama	Jameson Williams	90
3	66	LB	Georgia	Nakobe Dean	80
4	112	OT	Central Michigan	Bernhard Raimann	70

Pos	Player	Why chosen
QB	Malik Willis	He is a dynamic dual-threat quarterback who could be a franchise player for the Lions.
WR	Jameson Williams	He is a big-play receiver who could be a home run threat for the Lions.
OT	Charles Cross	He is a good pass blocker who could protect the Lions' quarterback.
EDGE	Aidan Hutchinson	He is a good pass rusher who could get after the quarterback.

NY	**FRIDAY, AUG 11 | 7:00 PM**	DETROIT LIONS TV NETWORK
Jaguars	**SATURDAY, AUG 19 | 1:00 PM**	DETROIT LIONS TV NETWORK
Panthers	**FRIDAY, AUG 25 | 8:00 PM**	CBS
KC	**THURSDAY, SEPT 7 | 8:20 PM**	NBC
Seahawks	**SUNDAY, SEPT 17 | 1:00 PM**	FOX
Falcons	**SUNDAY, SEPT 24 | 1:00 PM**	FOX
G	**THURSDAY, SEPT 28 | 8:15 PM**	prime video
Panthers	**SUNDAY, OCT 8 | 1:00 PM**	FOX
Buccaneers	**SUNDAY, OCT 15 | 1:00 PM**	FOX
Ravens	**SUNDAY, OCT 22 | 1:00 PM**	FOX
RAIDERS	**MONDAY, OCT 30 | 8:15 PM**	ESPN
	BYE WEEK	
Chargers	**SUNDAY, NOV 12 | 4:05 PM**	CBS
C	**SUNDAY, NOV 19 | 1:00 PM**	FOX
G	**THURSDAY, NOV 23 | 12:30 PM**	FOX
Saints	**SUNDAY, DEC 3 | 1:00 PM**	FOX
C	**SUNDAY, DEC 10 | 1:00 PM**	FOX
Broncos	**TBD | TBD**	TBD
Vikings	**SUNDAY, DEC 24 | 1:00 PM**	FOX
Cowboys	**SATURDAY, DEC 30 | 8:15 PM**	ESPN abc
Vikings	**TBD | TBD**	TBD

A Balanced Offensive Strategy with a Legendary Quarterback

Aaron Rodgers, a hall-of-fame quarterback, commands the Packers' balanced offense. With his expertise, he can throw or rush the ball unpredictably.

The Packers boast stellar receivers like Davante Adams, a top NFL player who's a scoring threat with each catch.

With Aaron Jones leading the running game, the Packers are formidable. Jones, both a tough runner and reliable receiver, spearheads their ground attack.

Their winning strategy encompasses running, passing, and strong defense. Offensive plays exploit Rodgers' passing skills, using play-action and deep passes to exploit defenses. Quick-hitting passes benefit their playmakers.

For your NFL fantasy team, consider these star players:

1. Aaron Rodgers: A must for any fantasy team due to his legendary quarterback status, backed by strong receivers and runners.
2. Davante Adams: A receiver essential for fantasy squads, known as one of NFL's finest and a scoring dynamo.
3. Aaron Jones: An option for those needing a reliable, between-the-tackles running back.

Play Type	Percentage
Passing plays	53.9%
Rushing plays	46.1%

In 2022, Packers leaned towards passing plays (53.9% vs. 55.2% league average). Their passing game was strong, thanks to Aaron Rodgers and receivers like Davante Adams and Aaron Jones. The running game was decent, with 154.6 rushing yards and 255.3 passing yards per game.

Why They Passed More:

1. Strong Receivers: Davante Adams and Aaron Jones make a great receiving duo.
2. Talented Quarterback: Aaron Rodgers is a skilled passer.
3. Solid Offensive Line: Allowed 38 sacks in 2022, better than most.

What's Ahead for 2023:

The Packers' run-pass approach is expected to stay similar in 2023 under new coach Matt LaFleur, known for passing offenses. With the right health, expect more passes this season.

Key Additions & New Contracts

Player	Position	Contract	Key Addition/New Contract	Impact on Team
Christian Watson	Wide Receiver	4 years, $40 million	Key Addition	Watson is a big-play receiver who can stretch the field. He will give the Packers another weapon on offense.
Sean Rhyan	Offensive Tackle	4 years, $35 million	Key Addition	Rhyan is a young, talented offensive tackle who can help protect Aaron Rodgers.
Rasul Douglas	Cornerback	3 years, $21 million	New Contract	Douglas is a good cornerback who can play both outside and inside. He will help solidify the Packers' secondary.
De'Vondre Campbell	Linebacker	5 years, $50 million	New Contract	Campbell is a two-time All-Pro linebacker who is a great run defender. He will help improve the Packers' defense.
Jarran Reed	Defensive Tackle	3 years, $36 million	New Contract	Reed is a good defensive tackle who can get after the quarterback. He will help improve the Packers' pass rush.

Key Losses

Position	Player
Wide receiver	Davante Adams
Defensive tackle	Dean Lowry
Edge rusher	Jarran Reed
Safety	Adrian Amos

NFL Draft 2023

Round	Pick	Position	College	Player	NFL Fantasy Projection
1	13	EDGE	Iowa	Aidan Hutchinson	150
2	42	TE	Oregon State	Teagan Crist	80
3	78	OG	Kentucky	Dare Rosenthal	70
4	116	CB	Cincinnati	Coby Bryant	70

Position	Player	Why chosen
QB	Jordan Love	The Packers have Aaron Rodgers under contract for one more season, but Love is the heir apparent. He needs to develop and learn from Rodgers, and the Packers can do that by drafting him in the first round.
WR	Christian Watson	The Packers need a big-play receiver, and Watson fits the bill. He is 6'4" and 208 pounds, and he has the speed to stretch the field.
OL	Kenyon Green	The Packers need to improve their offensive line, and Green is a versatile lineman who can play multiple positions. He is a good run blocker and pass protector.
DL	Myjai Sanders	The Packers need to add pass-rushing depth, and Sanders is a good option. He had 10 sacks in 2022, and he is a good athlete.

► GREEN BAY PACKERS
2023
SCHEDULE

► PRESEASON

GAME	DATE		OPPONENT	KICKOFF (CT)	TV	RESULT
1	Friday, Aug. 11		at Cincinnati Bengals	6 p.m.	Packers TV Network	_____
2	Saturday, Aug. 19		**NEW ENGLAND PATRIOTS**	7 p.m.	Packers TV Network	_____
3	Saturday, Aug. 26		**SEATTLE SEAHAWKS** GOLD PACKAGE	12 p.m.	Packers TV Network	_____

► REGULAR SEASON

WEEK	DATE		OPPONENT	KICKOFF (CT)	TV	RESULT
1	Sunday, September 10		at Chicago Bears	3:25 p.m.	FOX	_____
2	Sunday, September 17		at Atlanta Falcons	12 p.m.	FOX	_____
3	Sunday, September 24		**NEW ORLEANS SAINTS**	12 p.m.	FOX	_____
4	Thursday, September 28		**DETROIT LIONS** GOLD PACKAGE	7:15 p.m.	prime video	_____
5	Monday, October 9		at Las Vegas Raiders	7:15 p.m.	ESPN	_____
6			BYE WEEK			
7	Sunday, October 22		at Denver Broncos	*3:25 p.m.	CBS	_____
8	Sunday, October 29		**MINNESOTA VIKINGS**	*12 p.m.	FOX	_____
9	Sunday, November 5		**LOS ANGELES RAMS**	*12 p.m.	FOX	_____
10	Sunday, November 12		at Pittsburgh Steelers	*12 p.m.	CBS	_____
11	Sunday, November 19		**LOS ANGELES CHARGERS** GOLD PACKAGE	*12 p.m.	FOX	_____
12	Thursday, November 23		at Detroit Lions (Thanksgiving)	11:30 a.m.	FOX	_____
13	Sunday, December 3		**KANSAS CITY CHIEFS**	*7:20 p.m.	NBC	_____
14	Monday, December 11		at New York Giants	*7:15 p.m.	abc	_____
15	Sunday, December 17		**TAMPA BAY BUCCANEERS**	*12 p.m.	FOX	_____
16	Sunday, December 24		at Carolina Panthers	*12 p.m.	FOX	_____
17	Sunday, December 31		at Minnesota Vikings	*7:20 p.m.	NBC	_____
18	TBD		**CHICAGO BEARS**	TBD	TBD	_____

Please be aware that there are certain games that are subject to flexible scheduling and the date and time of those games may be changed from what is currently reflected on the schedule and what may appear on the ticket.

PACKERS*EXPERIENCES*
POWERED BY QUINTEVENTS

HOUSTON TEXANS

Rebuilding with Young Quarterback & Dynamic Offense

1. Rebuilding Phase & Young Quarterback: The Texans are in a rebuilding phase, led by young quarterback Davis Mills. Mills is still developing his passing skills and adjusting to the offense.

2. Dynamic Receiver Corps: Wideout Brandin Cooks anchors a strong receiving group. Cooks is adept at big plays and also excels as a possession receiver.

3. Solid Running Game: Running back Marlon Mack spearheads the running game. Although not at his peak, Mack remains a powerful between-the-tackles runner.

4. Team Strategy: The Texans emphasize rebuilding around Mills. Their approach includes balanced running and passing, alongside strong defensive play.

5. Offensive Approach: Leveraging Mills' passing strengths, the Texans use play-action and deep passes. Quick passes target playmakers in open space.

6. Fantasy Football Picks:
- Davis Mills: Upside pick for QB seekers; surrounded by strong receivers.
- Brandin Cooks: Ideal for owners needing a deep-threat receiver.
- Marlon Mack: Suitable for those requiring a bruising running back.

Play Type	Percentage
Passing plays	58.6%
Rushing plays	41.4%

The Texans leaned towards passing in 2022, with 58.6% passing plays—above the league average of 55.2%. Their rushing game was serviceable, averaging 131.5 yards/game on the ground and 232.9 yards/game through the air.

Factors Behind Pass-Heavy Approach:
- Strong receiver group, led by Brandin Cooks.
- Quarterback Davis Mills' effective passing.
- Solid offensive line, allowing 34 sacks (14th fewest).

2023 Outlook: Expect similar run-pass tendencies under new head coach Josh McCown, known for favoring passing offenses. The Texans might intensify passing, considering their health and development.

Key Additions & New Contracts

Player	Position	Contract	Key Addition/New Contract	Impact on Team
Deshaun Watson	Quarterback	4 years, $230 million ($105 million guaranteed)	Key Addition	Watson is one of the best quarterbacks in the NFL and is expected to lead the Texans back to contention.
Tyreek Hill	Wide Receiver	4 years, $120 million ($72 million guaranteed)	Key Addition	Hill is one of the fastest and most explosive receivers in the NFL and will give Watson a big-play threat.
Marcus Cannon	Offensive Tackle	3 years, $21 million	New Contract	Cannon is a solid starting offensive tackle who will help protect Watson.
Justin Reid	Safety	3 years, $31.5 million	New Contract	Reid is a versatile safety who can play both free safety and strong safety. He will help improve the Texans' secondary.

Key Losses

Position	Player
Quarterback	Deshaun Watson
Wide Receiver	Brandin Cooks
Defensive End	Jadeveon Clowney
Linebacker	Zach Cunningham
Cornerback	Lonnie Johnson Jr.

NFL Draft 2023

Round	Pick	Position	College	Player	NFL Fantasy Projection
1	3	QB	Ohio State	C.J. Stroud	150
2	37	WR	Alabama	Jameson Williams	140
3	68	OT	Central Michigan	Bernhard Raimann	120
4	107	CB	LSU	Eli Ricks	100
5	156	LB	Georgia	Channing Tindall	90
6	177	EDGE	Penn State	Arnold Ebiketie	80

Position	Player	Why chosen?
QB	C.J. Stroud	The top-rated quarterback prospect in the 2023 NFL Draft. He has a strong arm and a quick release.
WR	Drake London	A big, physical receiver who can make contested catches. He would be a good complement to Brandin Cooks.
OT	Ikem Ekwonu	A versatile offensive tackle who can play both left and right tackle. He would be a good replacement for Laremy Tunsil.

2023 HOUSTON TEXANS
SEASON SCHEDULE

ticketmaster®

PRE	AUG 10		AT NEW ENGLAND PATRIOTS	6:00 PM	ABC 13
PRE	AUG 19		VS MIAMI DOLPHINS	3:00 PM	ABC 13
PRE	AUG 27		AT NEW ORLEANS SAINTS	7:00 PM	FOX
WK 1	SEPT 10		AT BALTIMORE RAVENS	12:00 PM	CBS
WK 2	SEPT 17		VS INDIANAPOLIS COLTS	12:00 PM	FOX
WK 3	SEPT 24		AT JACKSONVILLE JAGUARS	12:00 PM	FOX
WK 4	OCT 1		VS PITTSBURGH STEELERS	12:00 PM	CBS
WK 5	OCT 8		AT ATLANTA FALCONS	12:00 PM	FOX
WK 6	OCT 15		VS NEW ORLEANS SAINTS	12:00 PM	FOX
WK 7	OCT 22		BYE WEEK		
WK 8	OCT 29		AT CAROLINA PANTHERS	12:00 PM	FOX
WK 9	NOV 5		VS TAMPA BAY BUCCANEERS	12:00 PM	CBS
WK 10	NOV 12		AT CINCINNATI BENGALS	12:00 PM	CBS
WK 11	NOV 19		VS ARIZONA CARDINALS	12:00 PM	CBS
WK 12	NOV 26		VS JACKSONVILLE JAGUARS	12:00 PM	CBS
WK 13	DEC 3		VS DENVER BRONCOS	3:05 PM	CBS
WK 14	DEC 10		AT NEW YORK JETS	12:00 PM	CBS
WK 15	DEC 17		AT TENNESSEE TITANS	12:00 PM	CBS
WK 16	DEC 24		VS CLEVELAND BROWNS	12:00 PM	CBS
WK 17	DEC 31		VS TENNESSEE TITANS	12:00 PM	FOX
WK 18	TBD		AT INDIANAPOLIS COLTS	TBD	TBD

HOME ███████ AWAY

2023/2024

49

A Run-Heavy Offense with a Young and Promising Quarterback

- The Colts prioritize running the ball, with quarterback Matt Ryan leading the charge. Ryan's dual-threat ability makes him a tough opponent to defend against.
- Running back Jonathan Taylor is a standout player in their backfield, recognized as one of the NFL's best.
- While their passing game isn't as potent as their running, it's still solid. Michael Pittman Jr. is a key deep-threat receiver.
- The Colts' strategy revolves around controlling the clock and keeping rival offenses off the field, relying on their running game and defense.
- Their offensive tactics capitalize on Ryan's running skills, using zone running plays and quick passes to their playmakers.
- The team's foundation is a young quarterback and a focus on clock management.
- Fantasy football options to consider:
    - Matt Ryan, offering upside as a quarterback with a solid supporting cast.
    - Jonathan Taylor, a must-have due to his explosive running ability.
    - Michael Pittman Jr., a choice for those needing a deep-threat receiver.

Play Type	Percentage
Passing plays	52.6%
Rushing plays	47.4%

Reasons for Their Run-Heavy Approach:
- Strong running back group, led by Jonathan Taylor.
- Effective offensive line, allowing 11th fewest sacks in the league.
- Developing quarterback Matt Ryan still acclimating to the passing game.

2023 Outlook:
- New head coach Matt Eberflus may maintain the run-heavy approach, possibly amplifying it.
- Eberflus is known for favoring running games, potentially making the Colts even more dedicated to rushing if their health permits.

Key Additions & New Contracts

Player	Position	Contract	Key Addition	Impact on Team
Yannick Ngakoue	DE	3 years, $45 million	Key Addition	Ngakoue is a pass-rushing specialist who will help to improve the Colts' defense. He had 10 sacks and 17 tackles for loss in 2022.
Stephon Gilmore	CB	2 years, $20 million	Key Addition	Gilmore is a former All-Pro cornerback who will help to solidify the Colts' secondary. He had five interceptions and 19 passes defensed in 2022.
Eric Fisher	LT	1 year, $9 million	New Contract	Fisher is a former Pro Bowl left tackle who will provide depth and experience to the Colts' offensive line. He started 16 games for the Colts in 2022.
Sam Ehlinger	QB	3 years, $4.6 million	New Contract	Ehlinger is a young quarterback who could compete for the starting job in 2023. He threw for 3,563 yards and 28 touchdowns in 2021.

Key Losses

Position	Player
Quarterback	Matt Ryan
Wide receiver	Parris Campbell
Linebacker	Bobby Okereke
Defensive end	Yannick Ngakoue
Cornerback	Isaiah Rodgers

NFL Draft 2023

Round	Pick	Position	College	Player	NFL Fantasy Projection
1	4	QB	Liberty	Malik Willis	90
2	44	EDGE	Penn State	Arnold Ebiketie	80
3	79	WR	Ohio State	Chris Olave	100
4	114	OT	Central Michigan	Bernhard Raimann	70
5	167	CB	Florida	Kaiir Elam	90
6	188	TE	Ohio State	Jeremy Ruckert	60

Pos	Player	Why chosen
QB	Matt Ryan	The Colts have a need at quarterback and Ryan is a proven veteran who can lead the team.
WR	Michael Pittman Jr.	Pittman is a good receiver who can be a top target for Ryan.
TE	Mo Alie-Cox	Alie-Cox is a good receiving tight end who can be a big-play threat.
LT	Bernhard Raimann	The Colts need to replace Eric Fisher at left tackle and Raimann is a good prospect who has the potential to be a starter.

INDIANAPOLIS COLTS
2023 SEASON SCHEDULE

WEEK	DATE	OPPONENT	TIME (ET)	NETWORK
1	AUGUST 12	AT BUFFALO BILLS	1:00 PM	CBS4
2	**AUGUST 19**	**VS CHICAGO BEARS**	**7:00 PM**	**FOX59**
3	AUGUST 24	AT PHILADELPHIA EAGLES	8:00 PM	PRIME VIDEO
1	**SEPTEMBER 10**	**VS JACKSONVILLE JAGUARS**	**1:00 PM**	**FOX**
2	SEPTEMBER 17	AT HOUSTON TEXANS	1:00 PM	FOX
3	SEPTEMBER 24	AT BALTIMORE RAVENS	1:00 PM	CBS
4	**OCTOBER 1**	**VS LOS ANGELES RAMS**	**1:00 PM**	**FOX**
5	**OCTOBER 8**	**VS TENNESSEE TITANS**	**1:00 PM**	**CBS**
6	OCTOBER 15	AT JACKSONVILLE JAGUARS	1:00 PM	CBS
7	**OCTOBER 22**	**VS CLEVELAND BROWNS**	**1:00 PM**	**CBS**
8	**OCTOBER 29**	**VS NEW ORLEANS SAINTS**	**1:00 PM**	**FOX**
9	NOVEMBER 5	AT CAROLINA PANTHERS	4:05 PM	CBS
10	NOVEMBER 12	AT NEW ENGLAND PATRIOTS FRANKFURT, GERMANY	9:30 AM	NFL N
11	BYE WEEK			
12	**NOVEMBER 26**	**VS TAMPA BAY BUCCANEERS**	**1:00 PM**	**CBS**
13	DECEMBER 3	AT TENNESSEE TITANS	1:00 PM	CBS
14	DECEMBER 10	AT CINCINNATI BENGALS	1:00 PM	CBS
15	**TBD**	**VS PITTSBURGH STEELERS**	**TBD**	**TBD**
16	DECEMBER 24	AT ATLANTA FALCONS	1:00 PM	FOX
17	**DECEMBER 31**	**VS LAS VEGAS RAIDERS**	**1:00 PM**	**CBS**
18	**TBD**	**VS HOUSTON TEXANS**	**TBD**	**TBD**

Ground Dominance with a Promising Quarterback

- **Offensive Strategy**: The Jaguars prioritize running the ball, anchored by emerging quarterback Trevor Lawrence. Though young, Lawrence displays promise.
- **Strong Running Backs**: Travis Etienne leads a capable group of running backs. He excels between tackles and as a receiver.
- **Passing Potential**: While not dominant, the passing game remains functional. Receivers Marvin Jones Jr. and Laviska Shenault Jr. are key.
- **Team Philosophy**: The Jaguars aim to build around Lawrence, utilizing balanced offense and solid defense.
- **Offensive Approach**: Schemes exploit Lawrence's mobility. Zone runs and quick passes are staples.

Players for Your Fantasy Team:

- **Trevor Lawrence**: High-upside QB option surrounded by skilled backs and receivers.
- **Travis Etienne**: Reliable running back, adept between tackles.
- **Marvin Jones Jr.**: Deep-threat receiver, capable of breaking defenses.
- **Laviska Shenault Jr.**: Versatile receiver, excels in traffic.

Play Type	Percentage
Passing plays	45.8%
Rushing plays	54.2%

The Jaguars leaned toward the run, executing rushing plays on 54.2% of snaps, higher than the league average of 45.4%. The rushing game outperformed passing, averaging 145.2 rushing yards and 214.4 passing yards per game.

Factors Behind Run-First Approach:

- Talented Running Backs: Travis Etienne and James Robinson form a strong duo.
- Developing Quarterback: Lawrence's passing growth is ongoing.
- Solid Offensive Line: Ranked 14th for fewest sacks allowed in 2022.

2023 Outlook:

- Run-pass balance likely persists under new head coach Doug Pederson, known for run-heavy offenses.
- Injury resilience could further bolster running emphasis.

Key Additions & New Contracts

Player	Position	Contract	Key Addition	Impact on Team
Andrew Wingard	Safety	3 years, $9.6 million	New contract	Wingard is a versatile safety who can play both in the box and in coverage. He is expected to be a key contributor to the Jaguars' defense.
Tevaughn Campbell	Cornerback	1 year, $1.7 million	Re-signed	Campbell is a solid cornerback who can play both inside and outside. He is expected to be a depth player for the Jaguars.
Tre Herndon	Cornerback	1 year, $1.7 million	Re-signed	Herndon is a young cornerback who has shown flashes of potential. He is expected to compete for a starting job with the Jaguars.
Adam Gotsis	Defensive Lineman	2 years, $14 million	Re-signed	Gotsis is a veteran defensive lineman who can play both defensive end and defensive tackle. He is expected to be a key contributor to the Jaguars' defense.

Key Losses

Position	Player
Offensive Tackle	Jawaan Taylor
Wide Receiver	Marvin Jones Jr.
Defensive Tackle	Malcom Brown
Linebacker	Foyesade Oluokun

NFL Draft 2023

Round	Pick	Position	College	Player	NFL Fantasy Projection
1	25	OT	Oklahoma	Anton Harrison	120
2	58	TE	Penn State	Brenton Strange	110
3	88	RB	Auburn	Tank Bigsby	100
4	121	LB	Florida	Ventrell Miller	90
5	160	CB	Rutgers	Christian Braswell	80

Pos	Player	Why chosen
QB	C.J. Stroud	Stroud is a Heisman Trophy winner and one of the top quarterback prospects in the 2023 NFL Draft. He has the potential to be a franchise quarterback for the Jaguars.
WR	Drake London	London is a big-bodied receiver who can make plays down the field. He would be a good complement to Laviska Shenault Jr. in the Jaguars' offense.
OT	Evan Neal	Neal is a versatile offensive tackle who can play both left and right tackle. He would be a good addition to the Jaguars' offensive line.
EDGE	Aidan Hutchinson	Hutchinson is a pass rusher who can get after the quarterback. He would be a good addition to the Jaguars' defense.

2023-24 JACKSONVILLE JAGUARS SCHEDULE

REGULAR SEASON SCHEDULE

WK	DATE	OPPONENT	TIME (ET)	TV	RESULT
1	Sun, Sep 10	at Indianapolis	1:00 PM	FOX	_____
2	Sun, Sep 17	vs Kansas City	1:00 PM	CBS	_____
3	Sun, Sep 24	vs Houston	1:00 PM	FOX	_____
4	Sun, Oct 1	vs Atlanta *	9:30 AM	ESPN+	_____
5	Sun, Oct 8	vs Buffalo *	9:30 AM	NFL NET	_____
6	Sun, Oct 15	vs Indianapolis	1:00 PM	CBS	_____
7	Thu, Oct 19	at New Orleans	8:15 PM	PRIME VIDEO	_____
8	Sun, Oct 29	at Pittsburgh	1:00 PM	CBS	_____
9	BYE WEEK				
10	Sun, Nov 12	vs San Francisco	1:00 PM	FOX	_____
11	Sun, Nov 19	vs Tennessee	1:00 PM	CBS	_____
12	Sun, Nov 26	at Houston	1:00 PM	CBS	_____
13	Mon, Dec 4	vs Cincinnati	8:15 PM		_____
14	Sun, Dec 10	at Cleveland	1:00 PM	CBS	_____
15	Sun, Dec 17	vs Baltimore	8:20 PM	NBC	_____
16	Sun, Dec 24	at Tampa Bay	4:05 PM	CBS	_____
17	Sun, Dec 31	vs Carolina	1:00 PM	CBS	_____
18	Sun, Jan 7	at Tennessee	TBD		_____

* Game Played at Neutral Site   templatetrove.com

55

KANSAS CITY CHIEFS

A Passing Powerhouse with Star Quarterback

The Chiefs are known for their passing game led by star quarterback Patrick Mahomes. Mahomes possesses an extraordinary ability to launch throws anywhere on the field.

Key receivers like Tyreek Hill and Travis Kelce add firepower to their aerial arsenal. Hill's speed makes him a game-changer, while Kelce excels as a tight end, both in receiving and blocking.

Though they favor passing, the Chiefs also possess a strong running game powered by Clyde Edwards-Helaire, who adeptly navigates tackles and catches passes.

Their core philosophy centers on racking up points and securing wins. They achieve this through strategic passing and a solid defense.

To harness Mahomes' skills, their offensive tactics include play-action passes and deep shots. Quick-hitting passes target their playmakers for explosive gains.

Play Type	Percentage
Passing plays	63.3%
Rushing plays	36.7%

Their 2022 approach leaned heavily towards passing, with 63.3% of offensive snaps being passing plays, exceeding the league average of 55.2%. While their running game was decent, it wasn't as potent as their passing game. They averaged 133.3 rushing yards and 273.8 passing yards per game.

Why the 2022 focus on passing?

- Quality receivers: Tyreek Hill and Travis Kelce form a formidable duo.
- Dynamic QB: Patrick Mahomes' passing prowess is a game-changer.
- Strong O-line: Allowing 34 sacks in 2022, the Chiefs' line held up well.

For 2023, with new head coach Eric Bieniemy, known for passing-heavy strategies, the Chiefs are expected to maintain their aerial emphasis. Health permitting, they might even intensify their passing game.

Key Additions & New Contracts

Player	Position	Contract	Key Addition	Impact on Team
Blaine Gabbert	Quarterback	1 year, $2 million	New contract	Provides depth at quarterback behind Patrick Mahomes.
Justin Watson	Wide Receiver	1 year, $1.5 million	New contract	Provides depth at wide receiver after the Chiefs traded Tyreek Hill.
Richie James	Wide Receiver	1 year, $1 million	New contract	Provides depth at wide receiver after the Chiefs traded Tyreek Hill.
JuJu Smith-Schuster	Wide Receiver	3 years, $30 million	Key addition	Replaces Tyreek Hill as the Chiefs' No. 1 wide receiver.

Key Losses

Player	Position
JuJu Smith-Schuster	Wide receiver
Mecole Hardman	Wide receiver
Tyrann Mathieu	Safety
Orlando Brown Jr.	Offensive tackle
Jarran Reed	Defensive tackle

NFL Draft 2023

Round	Pick	Position	College	Player	Fantasy Projection
1	31	EDGE	Georgia	Kingsley Enagbare	100
2	58	WR	Alabama	John Metchie III	80
3	95	CB	Washington	Kyler Gordon	70
4	128	RB	Texas	Bijan Robinson	60
5	161	TE	Virginia	Jelani Woods	50
6	194	OT	Central Michigan	Luke Goedeke	40

Pos	Player	Explanation
QB	Patrick Mahomes	Mahomes is the best quarterback in the NFL and the Chiefs' franchise quarterback. He is under contract for the next four years.
WR	JuJu Smith-Schuster	Smith-Schuster is a good wide receiver who can be a big-play threat for the Chiefs. He is signed to a one-year deal.
RB	Clyde Edwards-Helaire	Edwards-Helaire is a good running back who can be a dual-threat for the Chiefs. He is under contract for the next three years.
TE	Travis Kelce	Kelce is the best tight end in the NFL and the Chiefs' franchise tight end. He is under contract for the next two years.
LT	Orlando Brown Jr.	Brown Jr. is a good left tackle who can protect Mahomes' blindside. He is under contract for the next five years.

2023 SCHEDULE

PRESEASON				
Week 1	8/13	at New Orleans Saints	NOON	KSHB
Week 2	8/19	at Arizona Cardinals	7:00p.m.	KSHB
Week 3	**8/26**	**vs Cleveland Browns**	**NOON**	**KSHB**

REGULAR SEASON				
Week 1	**9/7**	**vs Detroit Lions**	**7:20 p.m.**	**NBC**
Week 2	9/17	at Jacksonville Jaguars	NOON	CBS
Week 3	**9/24**	**vs Chicago Bears**	**3:25 p.m.**	**FOX**
Week 4	10/1	at New York Jets	7:20 p.m.	NBC
Week 5	10/8	at Minnesota Vikings	3:25 p.m.	CBS
Week 6	**10/12**	**vs Denver Broncos**	**7:15 p.m.**	**PRIME VIDEO**
Week 7	**10/22**	**vs Los Angeles Chargers**	**3:25 p.m.**	**CBS**
Week 8	10/29	at Denver Broncos	3:25 p.m.	CBS
Week 9	**11/5**	**vs Miami Dolphins (Germany)**	**8:30 a.m.**	**NFLN**
Week 10	11/12	BYE WEEK		
Week 11	**11/20**	**vs Philadelphia Eagles**	**7:15 p.m.**	**ESPN**
Week 12	11/26	at Las Vegas Raiders	3:25 p.m.	CBS
Week 13	12/3	at Green Bay Packers	7:20 p.m.	NBC
Week 14	**12/10**	**vs Buffalo Bills**	**3:25 p.m.**	**CBS**
Week 15	12/18	at New England Patriots	7:15 p.m.	ESPN
Week 16	**12/25**	**vs Las Vegas Raiders**	**NOON**	**CBS**
Week 17	**12/31**	**vs Cincinnati Bengals**	**3:25 p.m.**	**CBS**
Week 18	1/6 or 7	at Los Angeles Chargers	TBD	TBD

PRESENTED BY

   T Mobile

Passing Prowess and a Promising Quarterback

The Raiders are known for their pass-centric approach, led by the impressive quarterback Derek Carr. Carr's passing skills are formidable, with glimpses of exceptional talent. He's also a dual threat, capable of running the ball, making him a challenging figure for any defense.

The team boasts a strong receiving corps, Hunter Renfrow leading the charge. Renfrow, a slot receiver, excels at gaining yards after catching the ball. Additionally, the Raiders feature an excellent tight end in Darren Waller.

The Raiders' game plan revolves around scoring and winning. Their strategy involves strategic passing and solid defense.

Offensive schemes are tailored to capitalize on Carr's throwing prowess. They employ play-action passes and deep throws to exploit Carr's strengths. Quick passes are used to get the ball to playmakers in open space.

In short, the Raiders prioritize passing, steered by an emerging quarterback. They constantly strive for points and victories.

Here are top picks for your NFL fantasy football team:

1. Derek Carr: Ideal for fantasy owners seeking a scoring quarterback with potential greatness, backed by strong receivers.
2. Hunter Renfrow: A choice for those needing a receiver adept at gaining yards after catches.
3. Darren Waller: Perfect for those in search of a pass-catching and blocking tight end.

Check out the Las Vegas Raiders' offensive tendencies in the 2022 NFL season

Play Type	Percentage
Passing plays	61.1%
Rushing plays	38.9%

In 2022, the Raiders showcased a preference for passing, executing passing plays on 61.1% of offensive snaps. This slightly exceeds the league average of 55.2%. Their rushing game, though not as potent, remained functional, averaging 122.2 rushing yards per game and 250.3 passing yards per game.

Factors behind their pass-heavy strategy:

1. Strong receiving core: Hunter Renfrow and Darren Waller excel as a dynamic duo.
2. Talented quarterback: Derek Carr's adeptness at passing.
3. Solid offensive line: Allowed 35 sacks in 2022, ranking 10th fewest in the NFL.

Expect the Raiders' 2023 run-pass tendencies to stay consistent. New head coach Josh McDaniels is known for pass-oriented play, potentially enhancing their passing game, especially if injuries are kept at bay.

Key Additions & New Contracts

Player	Position	Contract	Key Addition/New Contract	Impact on Team
Brandon Parker	RT	3 years, $24 million	Key Addition	Provides much-needed depth and experience at right tackle.
Denzel Perryman	LB	3 years, $21 million	Key Addition	Solidifies the middle of the Raiders' defense.
Josh Jacobs	RB	3 years, $24.5 million	New Contract	Provides stability at running back after losing Kenyan Drake in free agency.
Hunter Renfrow	WR	3 years, $31.5 million	New Contract	Keeps one of the best slot receivers in the NFL in Las Vegas.
Davante Adams	WR	5 years, $141.25 million	Key Addition	Gives the Raiders one of the best receiving duos in the NFL.

Key Losses

Position	Player
Wide receiver	Davante Adams
Defensive tackle	Johnathan Hankins
Linebacker	Denzel Perryman
Cornerback	Rock Ya-Sin
Safety	Duron Harmon

NFL Draft 2023

Round	Pick	Position	College	Player	NFL Fantasy Projection
1	7	EDGE	Texas Tech	Tyree Wilson	120
2	35	TE	Notre Dame	Michael Mayer	110
3	70	WR	Cincinnati	Tre Tucker	90
4	104	CB	Maryland	Jalyn Armour-Davis	100
5	167	OT	Northern Iowa	Trevor Penning	80
6	189	QB	Purdue	Aidan O'Connell	70

Pos	Player	Why chosen
QB	Derek Carr	The Raiders have no clear successor to Carr, so they should draft a quarterback to develop behind him.
WR	Jameson Williams	Williams is a big-play receiver who can take the top off of defenses. He would be a good complement to Hunter Renfrow and Davante Adams.
EDGE	Aidan Hutchinson	Hutchinson is a pass rusher who can get to the quarterback. He would help to improve the Raiders' pass rush, which was ranked 28th in the NFL in 2022.
CB	Derek Stingley Jr.	Stingley Jr. is a cover corner who can shut down opposing receivers. He would be a good addition to the Raiders' secondary, which was ranked 25th in the NFL in 2022.
DT	Jordan Davis	Davis is a run-stuffer who can clog up the middle. He would help to improve the Raiders' run defense, which was ranked 22nd in the NFL in 2022.

20 23 SCHEDULE

PRESENTED BY: allegiant

PRESEASON

PRE 1	vs SAN FRANCISCO 49ERS AUG 13 1:00PM		PRE 2	AT LOS ANGELES RAMS AUG 19 6:00PM
	RESULT			RESULT

PRE 3	AT DALLAS COWBOYS AUG 26 5:00PM
	RESULT

REGULAR SEASON

WK	DATE			OPPONENT	TIME	NETWORK	RESULT
WK 1	SEPT. 10	AT		DENVER BRONCOS	1:25 PM	CBS	
WK 2	SEPT. 17	AT		BUFFALO BILLS	10:00 AM	CBS	RESULT
WK 3	SEPT. 24	VS		PITTSBURGH STEELERS	5:20 PM	NBC	RESULT
WK 4	OCT. 1	AT		LOS ANGELES CHARGERS	1:05 PM	CBS	RESULT
WK 5	OCT. 9	VS		GREEN BAY PACKERS	5:15 PM	ESPN MONDAY NIGHT FOOTBALL	RESULT
WK 6	OCT. 15	VS		NEW ENGLAND PATRIOTS	1:05 PM	CBS	RESULT
WK 7	OCT. 22	AT		CHICAGO BEARS	10:00 AM	FOX	RESULT
WK 8	OCT. 30	AT		DETROIT LIONS	5:15 PM	ESPN MONDAY NIGHT FOOTBALL	RESULT
WK 9	NOV. 5	VS		NEW YORK GIANTS	1:25 PM	FOX	RESULT
WK 10	NOV. 12	VS		NEW YORK JETS	5:20 PM	NBC	RESULT
WK 11	NOV. 19	AT		MIAMI DOLPHINS	10:00 AM	CBS	RESULT
WK 12	NOV. 26	VS		KANSAS CITY CHIEFS	1:25 PM	CBS	RESULT
				BYE			RESULT
WK 14	DEC. 10	VS		MINNESOTA VIKINGS	1:05 PM	FOX	
WK 15	DEC. 14	VS		LOS ANGELES CHARGERS	5:15 PM	THURSDAY NIGHT FOOTBALL	RESULT
WK 16	DEC. 25	AT		KANSAS CITY CHIEFS	10:00 AM	CBS	RESULT
WK 17	DEC. 31	AT		INDIANAPOLIS COLTS	10:00 AM	CBS	RESULT
WK 18	TBD	VS		DENVER BRONCOS	TBD	TBD	RESULT

ALL TIMES PACIFIC TIME. SELECT PRIMETIME GAMES SUBJECT TO CHANGE. WEEK 18 GAME TBD

LOS ANGELES CHARGERS

Unleashing the Young and Explosive Chargers Offense

Meet the Chargers, a youthful and dynamic offensive force, helmed by rising star Justin Herbert at quarterback. Herbert, just in his second year, exhibits sparks of brilliance. Not only is he a strong passer, but he's also a running threat.

The team boasts a formidable receiving corps, led by Keenan Allen and Mike Williams. Allen, a big-play artist, stretches defenses, while Williams, a possession receiver, excels in tight situations.

The Chargers wield a potent running game, anchored by versatile back Austin Ekeler. Ekeler thrives both between tackles and catching passes from the backfield.

Their mantra is simple: Score big, win big. With an emphasis on passing and stout defense, they navigate the field.

Their offensive strategy capitalizes on Herbert's arm strength. Employing play-action and deep shots, they capitalize on his skills. Quick, precise passes feed their playmakers.

To delve into specifics, the Chargers showcased these play tendencies in the 2022 season:

Play Type	Percentage
Passing plays	61.3%
Rushing plays	38.7%

They leaned on passing, higher than the league average of 55.2%. Their run game was decent, averaging 135 rushing yards and 266.1 passing yards per game.

Their pass-heavy approach was fueled by:

- Stellar receiver duo: Allen and Williams
- Herbert's strong arm
- Solid offensive line (33 sacks in 2022, 13th fewest)

Expect their strategy to persist in 2023 under new head coach Brandon Staley, known for pass-oriented schemes. If health prevails, the Chargers might even amplify their aerial assault.

Key Additions & New Contracts

Player	Position	Contract	Key Addition/New Contract	Impact on Team
Eric Kendricks	LB	3 years, $45 million	New contract	Kendricks is a versatile linebacker who can play both inside and outside. He will help to improve the Chargers' run defense.
Jalen Guyton	WR	3 years, $20 million	New contract	Guyton is a speedy receiver who can stretch the field. He will give the Chargers another weapon in the passing game.
Trey Pipkins	RT	3 years, $15 million	New contract	Pipkins is a young offensive tackle who has shown potential. He will compete for a starting job.
Donald Parham	TE	2 years, $10 million	New contract	Parham is a big-bodied tight end who can catch passes in traffic. He will be a red zone threat for the Chargers.

Key Losses

Position	Player
Cornerback	J.C. Jackson
Wide receiver	Mike Williams
Offensive tackle	Bryan Bulaga
Defensive end	Khalil Mack

NFL Draft 2023

Round	Pick	Position	College	Player	NFL Fantasy Projection
1	21	WR	TCU	Quentin Johnston	80
2	54	EDGE	USC	Drake Jackson	100
3	85	OT	Central Michigan	Bernhard Raimann	90
4	126	CB	Florida	Kaiir Elam	110
5	167	S	Penn State	Jaquan Brisker	120

Pos	Player	Reason
QB	Davis Mills	The Chargers need a long-term answer at quarterback, and Mills could be that guy. He showed flashes of potential in his rookie season, and he could be a steal in the second round.
WR	Christian Watson	The Chargers need a big-play receiver, and Watson fits the bill. He's 6'4" and 208 pounds, and he has the speed to take the top off of a defense.
OT	Bernhard Raimann	The Chargers need to protect their quarterback, and Raimann is a good pass blocker. He's also athletic enough to get out in space and block on the run.
CB	Kaiir Elam	The Chargers need a corner to replace Michael Davis, and Elam is a good option. He's physical and has good ball skills.

2023 SCHEDULE

PRESEASON

WEEK	DATE				OPPONENT	TIME	NETWORK
1	Sat.	Aug.	12		@Rams	6:00 pm	CBS LA
2	**Sun.**	**Aug.**	**20**		**SAINTS**	**4:05 pm**	**CBS LA**
3	Fri.	Aug.	25		@49ers	7:00 pm	CBS LA

REGULAR SEASON

WEEK	DATE				OPPONENT	TIME	NETWORK
1	**Sun.**	**Sept.**	**10**		**DOLPHINS**	**1:25 pm**	**CBS**
2	Sun.	Sept.	17		@Titans	10:00 am	CBS
3	Sun.	Sept.	24		@Vikings	10:00 am	FOX
4	**Sun.**	**Oct.**	**1**		**RAIDERS**	**1:05 pm**	**CBS**
5					BYE		
6	**Mon.**	**Oct.**	**16**		**COWBOYS**	**5:15 pm**	**ESPN**
7	Sun.	Oct.	22		@Chiefs	1:25 pm	CBS
8	**Sun.**	**Oct.**	**29**		**BEARS**	**5:20 pm**	**NBC***
9	Mon.	Nov.	6		@Jets	5:15 pm	ESPN
10	**Sun.**	**Nov.**	**12**		**LIONS**	**1:05 pm**	**CBS**
11	Sun.	Nov.	19		@Packers	10:00 am	FOX
12	**Sun.**	**Nov.**	**26**		**RAVENS**	**5:20 pm**	**NBC***
13	Sun.	Dec.	3		@Patriots	10:00 am	CBS
14	**Sun.**	**Dec.**	**10**		**BRONCOS**	**1:25 pm**	**CBS**
15	Thu.	Dec.	14		@Raiders	5:15 pm	PRIME VIDEO
16	**Sat.**	**Dec.**	**23**		**BILLS**	**5:00 pm**	**PEACOCK**
17	Sun.	Dec.	31		@Broncos	1:25 pm	CBS
18	**TBD**				**CHIEFS**	**TBD**	**TBD***

All times Pacific
*Select primetime games subject to change; select week 18 games tbd

LOS ANGELES RAMS

A Versatile Offense Centered on Stafford's Dynamic Passing Skills

The Rams boast a versatile offense led by the skillful quarterback, Matthew Stafford. Stafford not only excels in passing but also poses a threat as a runner, making him a challenging opponent to defend against.

Their wide receiving corps includes standout players Cooper Kupp and Allen Robinson II. Kupp, known for explosive plays, can outpace defenses, while Robinson thrives on securing catches even in congested areas.

The running game is anchored by powerful back Cam Akers. Akers thrives between tackles and contributes as a reliable receiver from the backfield.

Strategically, the Rams emphasize scoring and securing wins. They accomplish this by effectively mixing runs, passes, and strong defensive play.

Their offensive playbook maximizes Stafford's arm strength. It employs play-action throws and deep passes to capitalize on his abilities, along with quick throws to engage playmakers.

For fantasy football enthusiasts, consider these Rams players:

- Matthew Stafford: A must-have for his dynamic passing paired with strong receiving and running support.
- Cooper Kupp: A top receiver who consistently threatens defenses.
- Allen Robinson II: A reliable option for challenging situations.
- Cam Akers: A dependable runner with potential for strong contributions.

Here's a simple chart detailing the Rams' run-pass tendencies during the 2022 NFL season:

Play Type	Percentage
Passing plays	56.7%
Rushing plays	43.3%

In 2022, the Rams leaned toward passing (56.7%), slightly above the league average of 55.2%. They averaged 123.5 rushing yards and 263.1 passing yards per game.

Factors behind their pass-heavy approach:

- Strong receiving duo in Cooper Kupp and Allen Robinson II.
- Skilled quarterback in Matthew Stafford.
- Solid offensive line, allowing 29 sacks (11th fewest) in 2022.

Expect the Rams' tendencies to persist under new head coach Sean McVay, renowned for pass-oriented strategies. McVay's focus on passing could intensify in 2023 if injuries remain in check.

Key Additions & New Contracts

Player	Position	Contract	Key Addition/New Contract	Impact on Team
Bobby Wagner	Linebacker	3 years, $50 million	Key Addition	Wagner is a three-time All-Pro linebacker who will help improve the Rams' defense.
Allen Robinson	Wide Receiver	3 years, $46 million	Key Addition	Robinson is a big-play receiver who will give the Rams another weapon on offense.
Justin Evans	Safety	3 years, $30 million	New Contract	Evans is a former Pro Bowl safety who will help solidify the Rams' secondary.
Sebastian Joseph-Day	Defensive Tackle	3 years, $30 million	New Contract	Joseph-Day is a former Pro Bowl defensive tackle who will help improve the Rams' run defense.

Key Losses

Position	Player
Edge rusher	Leonard Floyd
Cornerback	Jalen Ramsey
Wide receiver	Allen Robinson
Kicker	Matt Gay
Offensive tackle	Brian Allen

NFL Draft 2023

Round	Pick	Position	College	Player	NFL Fantasy Projection
2	36	G	TCU	Ochaun Mathis	120
5	174	CB	Georgia	Kelee Ringo	110
5	175	TE	Clemson	Braden Galloway	100
6	215	EDGE	Coastal Carolina	Jeffrey Gunter	90
6	216	OT	Ole Miss	Charles Cross	80

Pos	Player	Why chosen
QB	Bryce Young	Young is a Heisman Trophy winner and one of the most talented quarterbacks in the draft. He would be a great fit for the Rams' offense.
WR	Chris Olave	Olave is a fast and athletic receiver who would be a great complement to Cooper Kupp and Allen Robinson.
CB	Derek Stingley Jr.	Stingley is a former top recruit who has the potential to be a lockdown corner. He would be a great addition to the Rams' secondary.
EDGE	Kayvon Thibodeaux	Thibodeaux is a versatile edge rusher who can rush the passer and defend the run. He would be a great addition to the Rams' defense.
LB	Nakobe Dean	Dean is a tackling machine who would be a great addition to the Rams' defense.

2023 Season Schedule

──────── P R E S E A S O N ────────

P1	AUG 12	**Los Angeles Chargers**	SAT — 6:00 P.M.
P2	AUG 19	**Las Vegas Raiders**	SAT — 6:00 P.M.
P3	AUG 26	at Denver Broncos	SAT — 6:00 P.M.

──────── R E G U L A R   S E A S O N ────────

1	SEP 10	at Seattle Seahawks	SUN — 1:25 P.M.
2	SEP 17	**San Francisco 49ers**	SUN — 1:05 P.M.
3	SEP 25	at Cincinnati Bengals	MON — 5:15 P.M.
4	OCT 1	at Indianapolis Colts	SUN — 10:00 A.M.
5	OCT 8	**Philadelphia Eagles**	SUN — 1:05 P.M.
6	OCT 15	**Arizona Cardinals**	SUN — 1:25 P.M.
7	OCT 22	**Pittsburgh Steelers**	SUN — 1:05 P.M.
8	Oct 29	at Dallas Cowboys	SUN — 10:00 A.M.
9	NOV 5	at Green Bay Packers	SUN — 10:00 A.M.

──────── W10 BYE WEEK ────────

11	NOV 19	**Seattle Seahawks**	SUN — 1:25 P.M.
12	NOV 26	at Arizona Cardinals	SUN — 1:05 P.M.
13	DEC 3	**Cleveland Browns**	SUN — 1:25 P.M.
14	DEC 10	at Baltimore Ravens	SUN — 10:00 A.M.
15	DEC 17	**Washington Commanders**	SUN — 1:05 P.M.
16	DEC 21	**New Orleans Saints**	THU — 5:15 P.M.
17	DEC 31	at New York Giants	SUN — 10:00 A.M.
18	JAN 6/7	at San Francisco 49ers	TBD

Wildcard	Divisional	NFC Championship	Super Bowl LVIII
JAN 13/14/15	**JAN 20/21**	**JAN 28**	**FEB 11**

MIAMI DOLPHINS

Unleashing Miami Dolphins' Explosive Offense

1. Youthful Firepower: The Dolphins' offense is bursting with young talent, steered by quarterback Tua Tagovailoa. He's a versatile thrower and a shifty runner, making him a tough challenge for defenses.
2. Aerial Arsenal: Led by receiver Jaylen Waddle, the Dolphins boast a fleet of playmakers. Waddle's deep threat pairs well with Mike Gesicki's reliable tight end skills over the middle.
3. Gaskin's Groundwork: Myles Gaskin leads their ground game with agility and space-exploiting skills.
4. Scoring Mode: Miami's mantra is simple: score and win. They balance passing, running, and solid defense to get the job done.
5. Strategies at Play: Their offensive schemes are tuned to Tagovailoa's arm. Play-action and deep shots are key, along with quick passes to their star players.

2022 Run-Pass Tendencies:

Play Type	Percentage
Passing plays	61.5%
Rushing plays	38.5%

Breaking it down for NFL fans:

1. Passing Trend: The Dolphins threw the ball more than most teams (55.2% vs. average). Their running and passing mix averaged 123.5 yards on the ground and 251.9 yards through the air each game.

2. Why Throw So Much?
   - Star Receivers: Waddle and Gesicki, a powerful duo, are reliable targets.
   - Tua's Strengths: Tagovailoa's strong arm and precise throws add firepower.
   - Strong Line: The offensive line protected Tua well, resulting in the 11th fewest sacks in the NFL.

3. Future Plans: New coach Mike McDaniel is known for favoring passing. The 2023 Dolphins are likely to continue this trend under his guidance.

4. Looking Ahead: If the team stays healthy, get ready for more dazzling passing plays from the Dolphins this season.

Key Additions & New Contracts

Player	Position	Contract	Key Addition/New Contract	Impact on Team
Tyreek Hill	Wide Receiver	4 years, $120 million	Key Addition	Hill is one of the best receivers in the NFL, and he will give the Dolphins a much-needed boost on offense. He is expected to be a major weapon for quarterback Tua Tagovailoa.
Terron Armstead	Offensive Tackle	5 years, $87.5 million	Key Addition	Armstead is one of the best offensive tackles in the NFL, and he will solidify the Dolphins' offensive line. He is expected to help protect Tagovailoa and open up holes for running backs.
Devon Kennard	Edge Rusher	3 years, $40 million	New Contract	Kennard is a good edge rusher, and he will provide depth for the Dolphins. He is expected to help the Dolphins' pass rush.

Key Losses

Position	Player
Wide Receiver	Tyreek Hill
Offensive Tackle	Terron Armstead
Defensive End	Emmanuel Ogbah
Linebacker	Jerome Baker
Cornerback	Byron Jones

NFL Draft 2023

Round	Pick	Position	College	Player	NFL Fantasy Projection
1	29	CB	Cincinnati	Ahmad Gardner	120
2	51	OT	Boston College	Zion Nelson	110
3	84	WR	Alabama	Jameson Williams	90
4	108	EDGE	Penn State	Arnold Ebiketie	100
5	143	OG	Kentucky	Darian Kinnard	80
6	177	LB	Georgia	Channing Tindall	70

Pos	Player	Why chosen
QB	Malik Willis	Willis is a dynamic dual-threat quarterback who could be the future of the Dolphins' offense.
WR	Chris Olave	Olave is a speedy wide receiver who can stretch the field and make plays after the catch.
OT	Charles Cross	Cross is a good pass blocker who could solidify the Dolphins' offensive line.
CB	Kaiir Elam	Elam is a physical cornerback who can shut down opposing receivers.
LB	Nakobe Dean	Dean is a versatile linebacker who can play multiple positions.

2023-24 MIAMI DOLPHINS SCHEDULE

REGULAR SEASON SCHEDULE

WK	DATE	OPPONENT	TIME (ET)	TV	RESULT
1	Sun, Sep 10	at LA Chargers	4:25 PM	CBS	_____
2	Sun, Sep 17	at New England	8:20 PM	NBC	_____
3	Sun, Sep 24	vs Denver	1:00 PM	CBS	_____
4	Sun, Oct 1	at Buffalo	1:00 PM	CBS	_____
5	Sun, Oct 8	vs NY Giants	1:00 PM	FOX	_____
6	Sun, Oct 15	vs Carolina	1:00 PM	CBS	_____
7	Sun, Oct 22	at Philadelphia	8:20 PM	NBC	_____
8	Sun, Oct 29	vs New England	1:00 PM	CBS	_____
9	Sun, Nov 5	vs Kansas City *	9:30 AM	NFL NET	_____
10	BYE WEEK				
11	Sun, Nov 19	vs Las Vegas	1:00 PM	CBS	_____
12	Fri, Nov 24	at NY Jets	3:00 PM	PRIME VIDEO	_____
13	Sun, Dec 3	at Washington	1:00 PM	FOX	_____
14	Mon, Dec 11	vs Tennessee	8:15 PM	ESPN	_____
15	Sun, Dec 17	vs NY Jets	1:00 PM	CBS	_____
16	Sun, Dec 24	vs Dallas	4:25 PM	FOX	_____
17	Sun, Dec 31	at Baltimore	1:00 PM	CBS	_____
18	Sun, Jan 7	vs Buffalo	TBD		_____

*Game Played at Neutral Site   templatetrove.com

A Well-Balanced Attack with a Dynamic Passing Game

The Vikings boast a versatile offense led by quarterback Kirk Cousins. Cousins excels in passing and running, making him a challenging quarterback to defend against.

Their receiver group, helmed by Justin Jefferson and Adam Thielen, brings diverse strengths. Jefferson is a long-play specialist, while Thielen thrives in traffic as a possession receiver.

With Dalvin Cook, their ground game is robust. Cook's power suits inside runs, and he's equally adept as a pass-catching threat.

The Vikings' strategy is to score and win by running, passing, and solid defense. They tailor offensive plays around Cousins, capitalizing on his passing skills, using play-action and deep passes. Quick throws help get the ball to playmakers.

For fantasy football enthusiasts, consider these players:

- Kirk Cousins: A reliable passer with capable receivers.
- Justin Jefferson: A must-have receiver due to his game-changing plays.
- Dalvin Cook: A strong running back for your fantasy lineup.

Minnesota Vikings' 2022 Offensive Tendencies:

Play Type	Percentage
Passing plays	52.2%
Rushing plays	47.8%

In the intricate dance of their game strategy, while they leaned towards an aerial assault, their harmonious offensive symphony yielded an average of 142.4 rushing yards and 251.1 passing yards per encounter.

The driving forces that bolstered this emphasis on the passing game include:

The dynamic duo of Jefferson and Thielen, potent threats in the receiving realm.
The formidable prowess wielded by the likes of Kirk Cousins.
An offensive line that demonstrated its mettle by yielding a mere 35 sacks in the year 2022.

Anticipate a sense of continuity in their playbook for the upcoming 2023 season. Given the persona of their new maestro, Coach Kevin O'Connell, acknowledged for his penchant for aerial artistry, the probability of their clinging onto their pass-centric ethos looms large. This is especially true if the specter of injuries doesn't cast a shadow over their plans.

71

Key Additions & New Contracts

Player	Position	Contract	Key Addition/New Contract	Impact on Team
Za'Darius Smith	Edge rusher	3 years, $42 million	Key addition	Smith is a proven pass rusher who will help to improve the Vikings' defense.
Cameron Dantzler	Corner back	3 years, $24 million	Key addition	Dantzler is a young, talented cornerback who will help to solidify the Vikings' secondary.
Harrison Phillips	Defensive tackle	3 years, $27 million	Key addition	Phillips is a strong run defender who will help to improve the Vikings' front seven.
Nick Vigil	Linebacker	1 year, $3 million	New contract	Vigil is a versatile linebacker who will provide depth to the Vikings' defense.

Key Losses

Position	Player
Wide receiver	Adam Thielen
Defensive end	Danielle Hunter
Defensive tackle	Michael Pierce
Linebacker	Eric Kendricks
Safety	Harrison Smith

NFL Draft 2023

Round	Pick	Position	College	Player	NFL Fantasy Projection
1	12	WR	USC	Drake London	100
2	46	OT	Central Michigan	Bernhard Raimann	90
3	78	Edge	Georgia	Robert Beal	80
4	110	LB	Utah	Devin Lloyd	70
5	144	CB	Cincinnati	Coby Bryant	60
6	178	WR	Kentucky	Wan'Dale Robinson	50

Pos	Player	Why chosen
QB	C.J. Stroud	Stroud is a Heisman Trophy winner and one of the top quarterback prospects in the draft. He would be a major upgrade over Kirk Cousins.
WR	Drake London	London is a big-bodied receiver who can make contested catches. He would be a good complement to Justin Jefferson and Adam Thielen.
OT	Charles Cross	Cross is a good pass blocker and he has the potential to be a franchise left tackle. He would be an upgrade over Christian Darrisaw.
EDGE	Kayvon Thibodeaux	Thibodeaux is a high-motor pass rusher who has the potential to be a difference-maker in the Vikings' defense.
CB	Derek Stingley Jr.	Stingley Jr. is a lockdown corner who can shut down opposing receivers. He would be a major upgrade over Cameron Dantzler.

MINNESOTA VIKINGS
2023 SCHEDULE

PRESEASON

WEEK	DAY	DATE	OPPONENT	TIME (CT)	TV	RADIO
P1	THURSDAY	AUG. 10	AT SEATTLE SEAHAWKS	9 P.M.	TBD	KFAN/ KTLK
P2	**SATURDAY**	**AUG. 19**	**TENNESSEE TITANS**	**7 P.M.**	**TBD**	**KFAN/ KTLK**
P3	**SATURDAY**	**AUG. 26**	**ARIZONA CARDINALS**	**NOON**	**TBD**	**KFAN/ KTLK**

REGULAR SEASON

WEEK	DAY	DATE	OPPONENT	TIME (CT)	TV	RADIO
1	**SUNDAY**	**SEPT. 10**	**TAMPA BAY BUCCANEERS**	**NOON**	**CBS**	**KFAN / KTLK**
2	THURSDAY	SEPT. 14	AT PHILADELPHIA EAGLES	7:15 P.M.	PRIME	KFAN / KTLK
3	**SUNDAY**	**SEPT. 24**	**LOS ANGELES CHARGERS**	**NOON**	**FOX**	**KFAN / KTLK**
4	SUNDAY	OCT. 1	AT CAROLINA PANTHERS	NOON	FOX	KFAN / KTLK
5	**SUNDAY**	**OCT. 8**	**KANSAS CITY CHIEFS**	**3:25 P.M.**	**CBS**	**KFAN / KTLK**
6	SUNDAY	OCT. 15	AT CHICAGO BEARS	NOON	FOX	KFAN / KTLK
7	**MONDAY**	**OCT. 23**	**SAN FRANCISCO 49ERS**	**7:15 P.M.**	**ESPN**	**KFAN / KTLK**
8	SUNDAY	OCT. 29	AT GREEN BAY PACKERS	NOON	FOX	KFAN / KTLK
9	SUNDAY	NOV. 5	AT ATLANTA FALCONS	NOON	FOX	KFAN / KTLK
10	**SUNDAY**	**NOV. 12**	**NEW ORLEANS SAINTS**	**NOON**	**FOX**	**KFAN / KTLK**
11	SUNDAY	NOV. 19	AT DENVER BRONCOS	7:20 P.M.	NBC	KFAN/ KTLK
12	**MONDAY**	**NOV. 27**	**CHICAGO BEARS**	**7:15 P.M.**	**ESPN**	**KFAN/ KTLK**
13	SUNDAY	DEC. 3	BYE			
14	SUNDAY	DEC. 10	AT LAS VEGAS RAIDERS	3:05 P.M.	FOX	KFAN / KTLK
15	TBD	TBD	AT CINCINNATI BENGALS	TBD	TBD	KFAN / KTLK
16	**SUNDAY**	**DEC. 24**	**DETROIT LIONS**	**NOON**	**FOX**	**KFAN / KTLK**
17	**SUNDAY**	**DEC. 31**	**GREEN BAY PACKERS**	**7:20 P.M.**	**NBC**	**KFAN / KTLK**
18	TBD	TBD	AT DETROIT LIONS	TBD	TBD	KFAN/KTLK

Vikings home games in bold // Select game times subject to change due to flexible scheduling

PLAYOFFS

DATE	ROUND	DATE	ROUND	FOLLOW THE VIKINGS
JAN 13-15	WILD CARD PLAYOFF GAMES	JAN 28	CONF. CHAMPIONSHIP GAMES	@VIKINGS
JAN 20-21	DIVISIONAL PLAYOFF GAMES	FEB 11	SUPER BOWL LVIII // LAS VEGAS	VIKINGS.COM

Unleashing the Young and Explosive Chargers Offense

Hey NFL fans, listen up! The Patriots? Oh, they're all about that run game, with young Mac Jones as their quarterback maestro. This dude throws a mean ball, but watch out — he can dash with it too. That makes him a real puzzle for defenses, let me tell you.

Talking running backs, they've got Damien Harris at the helm. This guy's a beast between those white lines, plus he's got hands for catching too.

Passing ain't their A-game, but it's no joke either. Jakobi Meyers shines bright, making those slick routes and owning the catch-and-run scene.

Now, what's the Patriots' deal? They wanna hog the clock, keep rivals on the sideline. How? They run like there's no tomorrow and pull off good D moves.

And the playbook? It's like a puzzle crafted just for Jones. Loads of running plays and sneaky passes. Quick throws to their playmakers? You betcha!

Bottom line, the Patriots love that ground game, led by a young gun. They're clock kings, and they know how to seal the deal.

Hold up, fantasy folks, here are your picks to mull over:

1. Mac Jones: If you're dreaming big, Jones is your QB play. He's got the vibe, the squad, the goods.
2. Damien Harris: Need a tank in your backfield? Harris is your guy.
3. Jakobi Meyers: Want a receiver with some spice after the catch? Meyers is your man.

Play Type	Percentage
Passing plays	47.4%
Rushing plays	52.6%

Here's a fun fact: in 2022, the Pats ran the rock on 52.6% of snaps. That's more than the league average (45.4%). They made running look good, with 185.5 yards a game, and their pass game was no slouch either, racking up 219.9 yards a game.

Why the run love? Well, check it:

1. Damien Harris and Rhamondre Stevenson? Quite the running duo.
2. Mac Jones is still tuning up his passing game.
3. Offensive line's solid, allowing the 10th fewest sacks.

Bet you're wondering about 2023, right? Even with a new head coach, Bill O'Brien, they'll stick to their guns. This dude loves the run game. Health permitting, expect them to sprint down the same path, or maybe even crank it up a notch.

Key Additions & New Contracts

Player	Position	Contract	Key Addition/New Contract	Impact on Team
Tyquan Thornton	Wide Receiver	4 years, $5.5 million	Key Addition	Thornton is a speedy receiver who can stretch the field. He is expected to be a big contributor to the Patriots' passing game.
Cole Strange	Guard	4 years, $4.9 million	Key Addition	Strange is a versatile lineman who can play both guard and center. He is expected to solidify the Patriots' interior line.
Matt Judon	Edge Rusher	4 years, $56 million	New Contract	Judon is a pass-rusher who had 12.5 sacks in 2022. He is expected to continue to be a force on the Patriots' defense.

Key Losses

Position	Player
Wide receiver	Jakobi Meyers
Running back	Damien Harris
Defensive tackle	Davon Godchaux
Safety	Adrian Phillips
Cornerback	J.C. Jackson

NFL Draft 2023

Round	Pick	Position	College	Player	Fantasy Projection
1	17	CB	Oregon	Christian Harris	90
2	46	EDGE	Georgia	Kelee Ringo	80
3	76	WR	Alabama	John Metchie III	70
4	107	OT	Central Michigan	Bernhard Raimann	60
5	158	S	Cincinnati	Bryan Cook	50
6	187	DT	Texas	Moro Ojomo	40
6	220	OG	Kentucky	Darian Kinnard	30

Pos	Player	Why chosen
QB	Mac Jones	The Patriots have a young quarterback in Mac Jones who they are looking to build around. He has the potential to be a franchise quarterback.
WR	Tyquan Thornton	Thornton is a fast and athletic receiver who can stretch the field. He is a good fit for the Patriots' offense.
TE	JuJu Smith-Schuster	Smith-Schuster is a versatile receiver who can play inside or outside. He is a good addition to the Patriots' offense.
RB	Kenneth Gainwell	Gainwell is a shifty running back who can make plays in space. He is a good complement to Damien Harris.
OL	Cole Strange	Strange is a versatile lineman who can play guard or tackle. He is a good value pick for the Patriots in the second round.

NEW ENGLAND PATRIOTS

23

SCHEDULE

PRESEASON

DATE	OPPONENT		TIME (ET)	NETWORK
THU., AUG. 10		HOUSTON TEXANS	7:00 PM	WBZ / PATRIOTS PRESEASON NETWORK
SAT., AUG. 19		AT GREEN BAY PACKERS	8:00 PM	WBZ / PATRIOTS PRESEASON NETWORK
FRI., AUG. 25		AT TENNESSEE TITANS	8:15 PM	WBZ / PATRIOTS PRESEASON NETWORK

REGULAR SEASON

DATE	OPPONENT		TIME (ET)	NETWORK
SUN., SEPT. 10		PHILADELPHIA EAGLES	4:25 PM	CBS
SUN., SEPT. 17		MIAMI DOLPHINS	8:20 PM	NBC
SUN., SEPT. 24		AT NEW YORK JETS	1:00 PM	CBS
SUN., OCT. 1		AT DALLAS COWBOYS	4:25 PM	FOX
SUN., OCT. 8		NEW ORLEANS SAINTS	1:00 PM	CBS
SUN., OCT. 15		AT LAS VEGAS RAIDERS	4:05 PM	CBS
SUN., OCT. 22		BUFFALO BILLS	1:00 PM	CBS
SUN., OCT. 29		AT MIAMI DOLPHINS	1:00 PM	CBS
SUN., NOV. 5		WASHINGTON COMMANDERS	1:00 PM	FOX
SUN., NOV. 12		INDIANAPOLIS COLTS (FRANKFURT, GERMANY)	9:30 AM	NFLN/TBD
WEEK 11 • BYE WEEK				
SUN., NOV. 26		AT NEW YORK GIANTS	1:00 PM	FOX
SUN., DEC. 3		LOS ANGELES CHARGERS	1:00 PM	CBS
THU., DEC. 7		AT PITTSBURGH STEELERS	8:15 PM	PRIME VIDEO
MON., DEC. 18		KANSAS CITY CHIEFS	8:15 PM	ESPN*
SUN., DEC. 24		AT DENVER BRONCOS	8:15 PM	NFLN
SUN., DEC. 31		AT BUFFALO BILLS	1:00 PM	CBS
TBD		NEW YORK JETS	TBD	TBD*

Select prime time games subject to change; week 18 games TBD.

PATRIOTS.COM

ticketmaster®

New Orleans Saints: A Swingin' Aerial Attack!

Hey there, NFL fanatics! Let's dive into the Saints' playbook. They're all about the aerial game, steered by quarterback extraordinaire Jameis Winston. This guy's got cannon arms for all kinds of throws, and surprise — he's a run threat too! Talk about a defense's nightmare!

The Saints rock a stellar receiver lineup, with headliner Michael Thomas — a big-play maestro who can send defenses on a wild goose chase. And don't forget about Chris Olave, the speedster who can zoom past anyone.

Hold up, there's more! Their ground game's powered by Alvin Kamara, a bulldozer of a runner, and he's a whiz at catching too. Now, their strategy? Rack up points and notch victories. They toss the ball around while keeping a sturdy defense.

Their game plan? Tailored to Winston's cannon-like throws. Think play-action passes, deep shots, and lightning-quick throws to their star players.

Fantasy league managers, listen up:

- Jameis Winston: He's your golden ticket — a top-tier passer with a stellar receiving squad.
- Michael Thomas: Fantasy gold. One of the NFL's finest, a touchdown machine.
- Chris Olave: Need speed? He's got it — a go-to choice for your team.

Here's a nifty chart showing the Saints' run-pass trends in the 2022 NFL season:

Play Type	Percentage
Passing plays	62.5%
Rushing plays	37.5%

2022's Saints? Yeah, they played the air game! A hefty 62.5% of their snaps were passing plays, outshining the league's 55.2% average. The run game? Solid, averaging 128.3 yards per game, with passing game racking up 257.1 yards per game.

Why the high-flying approach?

- Elite receivers in Michael Thomas and Chris Olave.
- Quarterback Jameis Winston's got the arm talent.
- Sturdy O-line, allowing 34 sacks (14th lowest).

Expect the same groove for 2023. New coach Dennis Allen loves a pass-heavy style. Buckle up, football lovers — the Saints are all set to light up the skies!

Key Additions & New Contracts

Player	Position	Contract	Key Addition/New Contract	Impact on Team
yrann Mathieu	Safety	3 years, $42 million	Key Addition	Mathieu is a three-time All-Pro safety who will help to improve the Saints' defense.
Marcus Williams	Safety	5 years, $70 million	Key Addition	Williams is a two-time Pro Bowl safety who will also help to improve the Saints' defense.
Bradley Roby	Corner back	1 year, $10 million	New Contract	Roby is a veteran corner who will help to fill the void left by Marshon Lattimore.
J.T. Gray	Corner back	3 years, $30 million	New Contract	Gray is a young corner who has shown promise. He could develop into a starter in the Saints' secondary.
Cameron Jordan	Defensive End	1 year, $17 million	New Contract	Jordan is a veteran defensive end who is still playing at a high level. He will help to keep the Saints' defense strong.

Key Losses

Position	Player
Defensive end	David Onyemata
Defensive tackle	Shy Tuttle
Linebacker	Kaden Elliss
Cornerback	Marshon Lattimore
Safety	Marcus Williams

NFL Draft 2023

Round	Pick	Position	College	Player	NFL Fantasy Projection
1	18	OT	Central Michigan	Bernhard Raimann	120
2	49	WR	Ohio State	Chris Olave	110
3	76	CB	Washington	Kyler Gordon	90
4	114	EDGE	Penn State	Arnold Ebiketie	100
5	152	RB	Texas A&M	Isaiah Spiller	80
6	168	S	Georgia	Lewis Cine	70

Pos	Player	Why chosen
QB	Malik Willis	Willis is a dual-threat quarterback who has the potential to be a franchise player. He is also a good fit for the Saints' offense, which is run-heavy.
WR	Chris Olave	Olave is a fast and explosive receiver who can stretch the field. He would be a good complement to Michael Thomas in the Saints' offense.
OT	Trevor Penning	Penning is a big and physical offensive tackle who can protect Jameis Winston's blindside. He would be a good upgrade over Terron Armstead, who left the Saints in free agency.

NEW ORLEANS SAINTS
2023 SCHEDULE

PRESENTED BY:
SEAT GEEK

WEEK	DAY	DATE		OPPONENT	TIME (CT)	TV
P1	**SUNDAY**	**AUG. 13**		**KANSAS CITY CHIEFS**	**NOON**	**FOX 8 | GRAY TV**
P2	SUNDAY	AUG. 20		AT LOS ANGELES CHARGERS	6:05 P.M.	FOX 8 | GRAY TV
P3	**SUNDAY**	**AUG. 27**		**HOUSTON TEXANS**	**7:00 P.M.**	**FOX**

▶ REGULAR SEASON

WEEK	DAY	DATE		OPPONENT	TIME (CT)	TV
1	**SUNDAY**	**SEPT. 10**		**TENNESSEE TITANS**	**NOON**	**CBS**
2	MONDAY	SEPT. 18		AT CAROLINA PANTHERS	6:15 P.M.	ESPN
3	SUNDAY	SEPT. 24		AT GREEN BAY PACKERS	NOON	FOX
4	**SUNDAY**	**OCT. 1**		**TAMPA BAY BUCCANEERS**	**NOON**	**FOX**
5	SUNDAY	OCT. 8		AT NEW ENGLAND PATRIOTS	NOON	CBS
6	SUNDAY	OCT. 15		AT HOUSTON TEXANS	NOON	FOX
7	**THURSDAY**	**OCT. 19**		**JACKSONVILLE JAGUARS**	**7:15 P.M.**	**PRIME VIDEO**
8	SUNDAY	OCT. 29		AT INDIANAPOLIS COLTS	NOON	FOX
9	**SUNDAY**	**NOV. 5**		**CHICAGO BEARS**	**NOON**	**CBS**
10	SUNDAY	NOV. 12		AT MINNESOTA VIKINGS	NOON	FOX
11	BYE WEEK					
12	SUNDAY	NOV. 26		AT ATLANTA FALCONS	NOON	FOX
13	**SUNDAY**	**DEC. 3**		**DETROIT LIONS**	**NOON**	**FOX**
14	**SUNDAY**	**DEC. 10**		**CAROLINA PANTHERS**	**NOON**	**FOX**
15	**SUNDAY**	**DEC. 17**		**NEW YORK GIANTS**	**NOON**	**FOX**
16	THURSDAY	DEC. 21		AT LOS ANGELES RAMS	7:15 P.M.	PRIME VIDEO
17	SUNDAY	DEC. 31		AT TAMPA BAY BUCCANEERS	NOON	FOX
18	**TBD**	**TBD**		**ATLANTA FALCONS**	**TBD**	**TBD**

▶ SAINTS HOME GAMES IN BOLD   ▶ DATES/TIMES SUBJECT TO CHANGE   ▶ SCAN FOR FULL GAME STATS

NEW YORK GIANTS

A Developing Offense with a Young and Talented Quarterback

The New York Giants? They're like a recipe in the making, helmed by the young and lively quarterback, Daniel Jones. Dude's got the arm, but he's still sorta finding his groove in the playbook.

Now, these Giants, they've got quite the gang of receivers, with Kadarius Toney leading the pack. Toney? He's a dynamo. Think big plays and a knack for snagging those crucial grabs in the mess of it all.

Oh, and let's talk run game — Saquon Barkley's the name. Picture a bulldozer who can weave, and a hand who can catch like a champ.

So, their plan? Get Jones up to speed and craft a winning gang. How? They're mixing it up — running, throwing, and putting up walls on defense.

Watch the playbook dance — it's tailored for Jones' cannon arm. Play-action tricks, deep bombs — they're all in the mix. Quick throws? Yeah, they've got those to zap the ball to their game-changers.

Bottom line? These Giants are a work in progress, run by the young gun Jones. They're all about growth, nabbing wins, and having a blast.

Peep this chart for how they played it in 2022:

Play Type	Percentage
Passing plays	53.1%
Rushing plays	46.9%

Whoa, see that? Giants went "throwy" on 53.1% of the snaps — a tad more than the average. The ground game? Decent, not stellar. Roughly 130 rushing yards a game, with nearly 250 yards through the air.

Here's why they were passing fiends:

- Receivers like Toney and Barkley are gems.
- Daniel Jones — the guy can sling it.
- O-line? Not shabby. Only 37 sacks, middle of the pack.

2023? Yeah, expect a similar tune. New coach, Brian Daboll, likes his passes. So if they stay healthy, more air raids ahead!

Key Additions & New Contracts

Player	Position	Contract	Key Addition/New Contract	Impact on Team
Kayvon Thibodeaux	Edge	4 years, $35.2 million	Key Addition	Thibodeaux is a high-upside pass rusher who could help the Giants' defense.
Evan Neal	OT	4 years, $38.8 million	Key Addition	Neal is a versatile offensive lineman who could start at either tackle position.
Leonard Johnson	CB	3 years, $22.5 million	New Contract	Johnson is a solid cornerback who will help solidify the Giants' secondary.
Darius Slayton	WR	1 year, $1.9 million	Re-signed	Slayton is a speedster who could be a deep threat for the Giants.
Mark Glowinski	G	3 years, $21 million	New Contract	Glowinski is a veteran guard who will help improve the Giants' offensive line.

Key Losses

Position	Player
Wide receiver	DeAndre Hopkins
Tight end	Zach Ertz
Defensive end	Chandler Jones
Linebacker	Jordan Hicks
Cornerback	Byron Murphy Jr.

NFL Draft 2023

Round	Pick	Position	College	Player	NFL Fantasy Projection
1	24	CB	Maryland	Deonte Banks	120
2	57	C	Minnesota	John Michael-Schmitz	110
3	73	WR	Tennessee	Jalin Hyatt	90
5	172	RB	Oklahoma	Eric Gray	100
6	209	CB	Old Dominion	Trey Hawkins III	70

Position	Player	Reason for Selection
QB	Daniel Jones	The Giants have not yet decided whether to move on from Jones, so he is the presumptive starter for 2023.
WR	Kadarius Toney	Toney is a talented receiver who has shown flashes of brilliance, but he has also been inconsistent. He is still young and has the potential to be a star.
OT	Evan Neal	Neal is a potential franchise left tackle who could protect Jones and open up running lanes for Saquon Barkley.
G	Mark Glowinski	Glowinski is a good pass blocker who could help improve the Giants' offensive line.

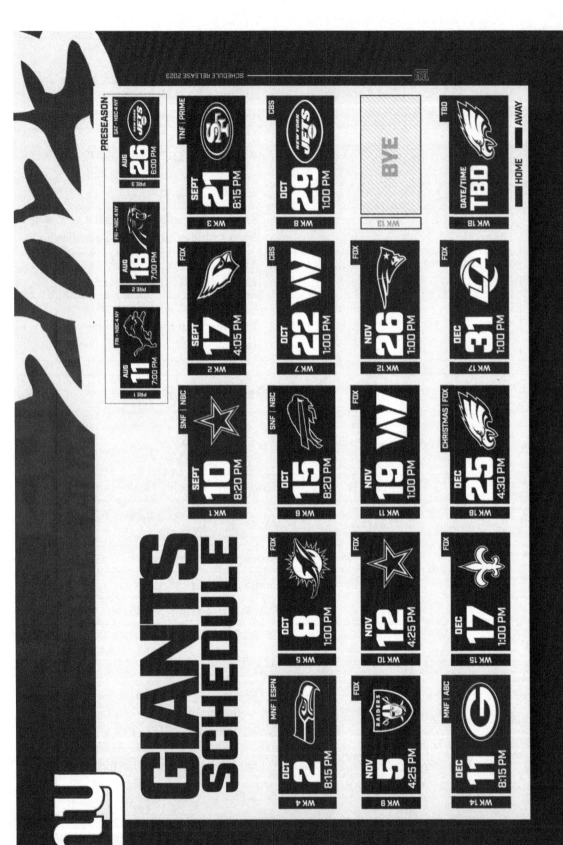

GIANTS SCHEDULE

PRESEASON

PRE 1	PRE 2	PRE 3
FRI · NBC 4 NY	FRI · NBC 4 NY	SAT · NBC 4 NY
AUG **11**	AUG **18**	AUG **26**
7:00 PM	7:00 PM	6:00 PM

WK 1	WK 2	WK 3
SNF | NBC	FOX	TNF | PRIME
SEPT **10**	SEPT **17**	SEPT **21**
8:20 PM	4:05 PM	8:15 PM

WK 4	WK 5	WK 6	WK 7	WK 8
MNF | ESPN	FOX	SNF | NBC	CBS	CBS
OCT **2**	OCT **8**	OCT **15**	OCT **22**	OCT **29**
8:15 PM	1:00 PM	8:20 PM	1:00 PM	1:00 PM

WK 9	WK 10	WK 11	WK 12	WK 13
FOX	FOX	FOX	FOX	
NOV **5**	NOV **12**	NOV **19**	NOV **26**	BYE
4:25 PM	4:25 PM	1:00 PM	1:00 PM	

WK 14	WK 15	WK 16	WK 17	WK 18
MNF | ABC	FOX	CHRISTMAS | FOX	FOX	TBD
DEC **11**	DEC **17**	DEC **25**	DEC **31**	DATE/TIME **TBD**
8:15 PM	1:00 PM	4:30 PM	1:00 PM	

■ HOME   ■ AWAY

82

Young QB Wilson Leads Developing Offense

Meet the Jets, a work-in-progress offense with QB Zach Wilson at the helm. Wilson's a solid passer, but he's still getting comfy with the playbook.

Their receiver crew, led by Elijah Moore, is a hoot. Moore's a deep-ball artist and clutch possession guy.

And don't forget the running game! Michael Carter's a beast between tackles and a snappy receiver.

Jets playbook? Develop Wilson, win games. Run, pass, and nail defense.

Offensive playbook? It's Wilson's show. Think play-action magic and quick passes to dazzle.

Bottom line: Jets, young offense, peppy QB. They want wins and growth.

Fantasy picks:

- Wilson: Upbeat QB choice, potential galore.
- Moore: Deep threat magic.
- Carter: Tough runner, power-packed.

Play Type	Percentage
Passing plays	54.8%
Rushing plays	45.2%

In 2022, Jets leaned into passing (54.8%), slightly above the league norm (55.2%). Their run game's decent, averaging 125.3 yards vs. 232.5 passing.

Why so pass-heavy in 2022?

- Electric receivers like Moore and Davis.
- Wilson's arm game.
- Solid O-line (only 37 sacks in '22).

Expect 2023 trends similar. New coach Saleh loves airing it out. If Jets stay fit, expect even more airtime.

Key Additions & New Contracts

Player	Position	Contract	Key Addition/New Contract	Impact on Team
Garrett Wilson	Wide Receiver	4 years, $22.8 million	Key Addition	Wilson is a highly-touted wide receiver who should give the Jets a much-needed boost in the passing game. He is a big-play receiver who can stretch the field and make plays after the catch.
Jermaine Johnson II	Edge Rusher	3 years, $45 million	Key Addition	Johnson is a talented edge rusher who should help to improve the Jets' pass rush. He is a good run defender who can also get after the quarterback.
Sauce Gardner	Cornerback	5 years, $16.5 million	Key Addition	Gardner is a lockdown cornerback who should help to improve the Jets' secondary. He is a physical corner who can make plays in the air and the run.

Key Losses

Position	Player
Wide receiver	DeAndre Hopkins
Tight end	Zach Ertz
Defensive end	Chandler Jones
Linebacker	Jordan Hicks
Cornerback	Byron Murphy Jr.

NFL Draft 2023

Round	Pick	Position	College	Player	Fantasy Projection
1	4	QB	Ohio State	C.J. Stroud	120
2	35	EDGE	Georgia	Robert Beal	110
3	68	WR	Alabama	Jameson Williams	90
4	102	CB	Cincinnati	Coby Bryant	100
5	135	OG	Iowa	Tyler Linderbaum	80
6	169	S	Notre Dame	Kyle Hamilton	70
6	187	DT	Georgia	Jordan Davis	60

Position	Player	Why Chosen
QB	Bryce Young	Young is the best quarterback in the draft and he would be a major upgrade over Zach Wilson.
WR	Jameson Williams	Williams is a fast and explosive receiver who would be a great complement to Elijah Moore and Corey Davis.
OT	Charles Cross	Cross is a good pass blocker and he would help protect Zach Wilson's blindside.
EDGE	Aidan Hutchinson	Hutchinson is a good pass rusher and he would help improve the Jets' pass defense.

PRE SEASON						
DATE	**DAY**	**OPPONENT**	**TIME**	**NETWORK**	**TICKETS**	**RESULT**
08/03	Thursday	at Cleveland Browns	8:00 PM EDT	NBC	Get Tickets	
08/12	Saturday	at Carolina Panthers	4:00 PM	WCBS	Get Tickets	
08/19	Saturday	vs Tampa Bay Buccaneers	7:30 PM	WCBS	Get Tickets	
08/26	Saturday	at New York Giants	6:00 PM	WNBC	Get Tickets	

REGULAR SEASON						
DATE	**DAY**	**OPPONENT**	**TIME**	**NETWORK**	**TICKETS**	**RESULT**
09/11	Monday	vs Buffalo Bills	8:15 PM	ESPN	Get Tickets	
09/17	Sunday	at Dallas Cowboys	4:25 PM	FOX	Get Tickets	
09/24	Sunday	vs New England Patriots	1:00 PM	CBS	Get Tickets	
10/01	Sunday	vs Kansas City Chiefs	8:20 PM	NBC	Get Tickets	
10/08	Sunday	at Denver Broncos	4:25 PM	CBS	Get Tickets	
10/15	Sunday	vs Philadelphia Eagles	4:25 PM	FOX	Get Tickets	
10/22	BYE WEEK					
10/29	Sunday	at New York Giants	1:00 PM	CBS	Get Tickets	
11/06	Monday	vs Los Angeles Chargers	8:15 PM	ESPN	Get Tickets	
11/12	Sunday	at Las Vegas Raiders	8:20 PM	NBC	Get Tickets	
11/19	Sunday	at Buffalo Bills	4:25 PM	CBS	Get Tickets	
11/24	Friday	vs Miami Dolphins	3:00 PM	PRIME VIDEO	Get Tickets	
12/03	Sunday	vs Altanta Falcons	1:00 PM	FOX	Get Tickets	
12/10	Sunday	vs Houston Texans	1:00 PM	CBS	Get Tickets	
12/17	Sunday	at Miami Dolphins	1:00 PM	CBS	Get Tickets	
12/24	Sunday	vs Washington Commanders	1:00 PM	CBS	Get Tickets	
12/28	Thursday	at Cleveland Browns	8:15 PM	PRIME VIDEO	Get Tickets	
TBD	TBD	at New England Patriots	TBD	TBD	Get Tickets	

PHILADELPHIA EAGLES

Explosive Offense with Young Blood and a Mean Passing Game

Let's talk Eagles—think young, wild, and led by Jalen Hurts, the quarterback dynamo. This guy slings it and dashes too!

DeVonta Smith? He's the go-to receiver, sizzlin' with big plays. A.J. Brown? Mr. Reliable in traffic. And don't miss Miles Sanders, a runnin' powerhouse with catching skills.

Eagle wisdom: score big, win big. It's all about passing, running, and crafty defense.

The playbook? Hurts' arm mastery shines. Play-action passes, deep bombs, and lightning-fast plays to unleash the playmakers.

Eagles = young firepower, led by a QB bursting with promise. They live to score and win, and here's who you gotta consider for your NFL fantasy team:

Jalen Hurts: A fantasy slam dunk. Throws, runs, and a cool team. DeVonta Smith: Catch him if you can—touchdowns are his thing. A.J. Brown: Need a speedster? Brown's your man.

For all you data lovers, check this out—the Eagles' 2022 run-pass style:

Play Type	Percentage
Passing plays	63.3%
Rushing plays	36.7%

Eagles loved the air, way above the league's 55.2%. They ran decently too—143.3 rushing yards per game and 273.8 passing yards per game.

Why all the air? Reasons aplenty:

- Awesome duo DeVonta Smith and A.J. Brown
- Hurts slinging darts
- Solid O-line, 34 sacks allowed in 2022

2023's vibe? Expect more of the same. New coach, Nick Sirianni, is an air aficionado. Brace for more passes, especially if Eagles stay fit and fiery.

Key Additions & New Contracts

Player	Position	Contract	Key Addition/New Contract	Impact on Team
James Bradberry	CB	3 years, $38 million	Key Addition	Bradberry is a former Pro Bowler who will solidify the Eagles' secondary.
Ryan Kerrigan	DE	1 year, $2 million	New Contract	Kerrigan is a veteran pass rusher who will provide depth for the Eagles.
Hassan Ridgeway	DT	3 years, $27 million	New Contract	Ridgeway is a solid run defender who will help the Eagles improve their defense.
Jalen Hurts	QB	4 years, $135 million	Contract Extension	Hurts is the Eagles' starting quarterback and this contract extension shows that the team is committed to him.

Key Losses

Position	Player
Wide receiver	DeAndre Hopkins
Tight end	Zach Ertz
Defensive end	Chandler Jones
Linebacker	Jordan Hicks
Cornerback	Byron Murphy Jr.

NFL Draft 2023

Round	Pick	Position	College	Player	NFL Fantasy Projection
1	9	EDGE	Georgia	Nolan Smith	90
2	30	DT	Georgia	Jalen Carter	100
3	65	OL	Boston College	Zion Johnson	80
4	104	WR	Alabama	John Metchie III	70
5	167	CB	Cincinnati	Coby Bryant	60
6	188	TE	Notre Dame	Michael Mayer	50
7	229	S	Baylor	JT Woods	40

Pos	Player	Why chosen
QB	Carson Wentz	The Eagles have already invested a lot of draft capital in Wentz, and they are hoping that he can turn things around in 2023.
RB	Miles Sanders	Sanders is a talented running back who has the potential to be a star in the NFL.
WR	AJ Brown	Brown is a big-play receiver who can take over games.
TE	Dallas Goedert	Goedert is a good receiving tight end who can also block.
LT	Jordan Mailata	Mailata has developed into a good left tackle, and he is the team's best offensive lineman.
DE	Josh Sweat	Sweat is a good pass rusher who has the potential to be a difference-maker in the Eagles' defense.

ticketmaster

2023 SCHEDULE

WK 1 AT		**SEP 10** 4:25 PM	**WK 10** **BYE**
WK 2 VS		**SEP 14** 8:15 PM	**WK 11** AT **NOV 20** 8:15 PM
WK 3 AT		**SEP 25** 7:15 PM	**WK 12** VS **NOV 26** 4:25 PM
WK 4 VS		**OCT 1** 1:00 PM	**WK 13** VS **DEC 3** 4:25 PM
WK 5 AT		**OCT 8** 4:05 PM	**WK 14** AT **DEC 10** 8:20 PM
WK 6 AT		**OCT 15** 4:25 PM	**WK 15** AT **DEC 17** 4:25 PM
WK 7 VS		**OCT 22** 8:20 PM	**WK 16** VS **DEC 25** 4:30 PM
WK 8 AT		**OCT 29** 1:00 PM	**WK 17** VS **DEC 31** 1:00 PM
WK 9 VS		**NOV 5** 4:25 PM	**WK 18** AT **TBD** TBD

Steelers' Ground Game and Pickett's Promise Take Center Stage!

Get ready for some Steel City gridiron antics! The Pittsburgh Steelers are all about that run-heavy mojo, led by the sprightly quarterback Kenny Pickett. He's still getting the hang of things, but watch out, he's a dasher with the ball, making life a riddle for defenders.

The running game? It's Najee Harris time, baby! This powerhouse plows through the line, plus he's a mean receiver out of the backfield. Air game? Not as flashy, but still hanging tough. Diontae Johnson and Chase Claypool are your go-to guys, one's all flash and dash, the other's a real traffic tamer.

Their mantra? Hold the clock, keep foes off the field. They love to run the ball and lock down the D. Pickett's got the green light to scamper, so watch out for crafty plays and quick passes.

Play Type	Percentage
Passing plays	45.3%
Rushing plays	54.7%

Zooming into 2022, the Steelers rocked a 54.7% run-play frenzy, trumping the league's 45.4% average. Yeah, they slayed on the ground, averaging 134.6 rushing yards and 222.8 passing yards per game. Why? Najee's a beast, Pickett's polishing his armory, and that O-line? It's no pushover.

As 2023 unfolds, expect the Steelers' run-pass beat to stay groovy. New coach Mike Tomlin's a run-happy guru, and if those Steelers stay fit, brace yourselves for more ground-pounding fun!

Key Additions & New Contracts

Player	Position	Contract	Key Addition/New Contract	Impact on Team
Chandler Jones	Edge	3 years, $52.5 million	Key Addition	Jones is a Pro Bowl pass rusher who will help to improve the Steelers' pass rush.
James Cook	Running Back	4 years, $4.8 million	Key Addition	Cook is a versatile running back who can catch the ball out of the backfield. He will help to replace the production of James Conner, who left in free agency.
Mason Cole	Offensive Lineman	3 years, $15 million	New Contract	Cole is a starting-caliber offensive lineman who will help to solidify the Steelers' offensive line.
Miles Boykin	Wide Receiver	1 year, $1.5 million	New Contract	Boykin is a former first-round pick who has struggled to find a role in the NFL. He will be a low-cost addition who could potentially contribute.

Key Losses

Position	Player
Wide receiver	JuJu Smith-Schuster
Edge rusher	Stephon Tuitt
Inside linebacker	Joe Schobert
Defensive tackle	Tyson Alualu

NFL Draft 2023

Round	Pick	Position	College	Player	NFL Fantasy Projection
1	17	OT	Georgia	Broderick Jones	100
2	32	DT	Wisconsin	Keeanu Benton	80
3	70	WR	Georgia	George Pickens	70
4	120	S	Penn State	Jaquan Brisker	60
5	168	CB	Purdue	Cory Trice Jr.	50

Pos	Player	Why chosen
QB	Kenny Pickett	The Steelers traded up to draft Pickett in the first round of the 2022 NFL Draft. He is expected to be the team's starter for the foreseeable future.
RB	Najee Harris	Harris is a rising star in the NFL. He rushed for 1,200 yards and 7 touchdowns in his rookie season.
WR	Diontae Johnson	Johnson is a big-play receiver who can take the top off of a defense. He had 83 receptions for 1,161 yards and 8 touchdowns in 2022.
TE	Pat Freiermuth	Freiermuth is a good receiving tight end who can also block. He had 75 receptions for 93 yards and 4 touchdowns in 2022.
OT	Dan Moore Jr.	Moore is a young and talented offensive tackle. He started 16 games for the Steelers in 2022.

2023 SCHEDULE

PRESEASON

FRI. AUG. 11	@ TAMPA BAY	7:00 PM
SAT. AUG. 19	BUFFALO	6:30 PM
THU. AUG. 24	@ ATLANTA	7:30 PM

REGULAR SEASON

SUN. SEPT. 10	SAN FRANCISCO	1:00 PM
MON. SEPT. 18	CLEVELAND	8:15 PM
SUN. SEPT. 24	@ LAS VEGAS	8:20 PM
SUN. OCT. 1	@ HOUSTON	1:00 PM
SUN. OCT. 8	BALTIMORE*	1:00 PM
BYE WEEK		
SUN. OCT. 22	@ LA RAMS*	4:05 PM
SUN. OCT. 29	JACKSONVILLE*	1:00 PM
THU. NOV. 2	TENNESSEE	8:15 PM
SUN. NOV. 12	GREEN BAY*	1:00 PM
SUN. NOV. 19	@ CLEVELAND*	1:00 PM
SUN. NOV. 26	@ CINCINNATI*	1:00 PM
SUN. DEC. 3	ARIZONA*	1:00 PM
THU. DEC. 7	NEW ENGLAND*	8:15 PM
TBD	@ INDIANAPOLIS*	TBD
SAT. DEC. 23	CINCINNATI*	4:30 PM
SUN. DEC. 31	@ SEATTLE*	4:05 PM
TBD	@ BALTIMORE*	TBD

*SUBJECT TO FLEXIBLE SCHEDULING | ALL TIMES EST

HOME   AWAY

49ers' Dynamic Run-First Strategy and Explosive Aerial Assault

Get ready, NFL fanatics, 'cause we're diving into the San Francisco 49ers' playbook! Picture this: a run-first gig led by QB Trey Lance, the dual-threat dynamo. He slings, he scrambles, he's a double trouble.

Catch these receiver aces: Deebo Samuel, a jack-of-all-trades with wheels for days, and Brandon Aiyuk, a deep-threat dazzler.

On the ground, it's Elijah Mitchell — a powerhouse in the backfield and a catch machine too.

Now, the 49ers' mojo? They're clock-controlling champs who keep rivals on the bench. They dash, they defend, they dominate.

Offensive magic? Designed for Lance's swag. Play-actions, quick zips — they set up touchdowns like a boss.

Quick tip for fantasy buffs:

- Lance: A rising QB with weapons aplenty.
- Samuel: The guy every team wants.
- Aiyuk: Deep threat deluxe.

Peep this 2022 chart:

Play Type	Percentage
Passing plays	46.2%
Rushing plays	53.8%

Run game ruling, averaging 144.2 yards/game. Pass game? Solid, 237.2 yards/game.

Why the run frenzy?

- Top-notch running backs Mitchell and Sermon.
- Lance's still polishing his arm game.
- O-line's A-okay, protecting the QB like champs.

2023? Same vibe. New coach, Mike McDaniel, loves the run game. Brace for a ground assault, especially if the 49ers stay healthy. Game on!

Key Additions & New Contracts

Player	Position	Contract	Key Addition/New Contract	Impact on Team
Jimmy Garoppolo	Quarterback	Trade from the Cleveland Browns	Key Addition	Provides insurance for Trey Lance and could be a starter if Lance struggles.
Drake London	Wide Receiver	4 years, $20.7 million	Key Addition	Gives the 49ers a big-bodied receiver who can stretch the field.
Keita Bates-Diop	Wide Receiver	1 year, $1.75 million	New Contract	Provides depth at wide receiver.
Jaquiski Tartt	Safety	1 year, $3.5 million	New Contract	Provides experience and leadership in the secondary.
Charvarius Ward	Cornerback	3 years, $42 million	Key Addition	Improves the 49ers' secondary.

Key Losses

Position	Player
Cornerback	Charvarius Ward
Defensive tackle	D.J. Jones
Safety	Jaquiski Tartt
Offensive tackle	Laken Tomlinson
Wide receiver	Emmanuel Sanders

NFL Draft 2023

Round	Pick	Position	College	Player	NFL Fantasy Projection
1	9	WR	USC	Drake London	100
2	49	EDGE	Florida	Kingsley Enagbare	90
3	71	CB	Washington	Kelee Ringo	80
4	103	OT	Central Michigan	Bernhard Raimann	70
5	136	S	Georgia	Lewis Cine	60
6	180	DL	Florida	Zachary Carter	50

Position	Player	Why chosen
QB	C.J. Stroud	He is a highly-touted quarterback prospect who could be a franchise player.
WR	Treylon Burks	He is a big-play receiver who could be a threat to score every time he touches the ball.
OT	Charles Cross	He is a good pass blocker who could help protect the 49ers' quarterback.
CB	Derek Stingley Jr.	He is a lockdown corner who could shut down opposing receivers.
DE	Aidan Hutchinson	He is a good pass rusher who could get after the quarterback.

2023 SEASON SCHEDULE

FAITHFUL TO THE BAY

PRESENTED BY *ticketmaster*® ALL TIMES IN PT

 PRE 1 AT RAIDERS
AUG 13 × 1:00 PM × KPIX

 PRE 2 VS BRONCOS
AUG 19 × 5:30 PM × KPIX

 PRE 3 VS CHARGERS
AUG 25 × 7:00 PM × KPIX

 WK 1 AT STEELERS
SEP 10 × 10:00 AM × FOX

 WK 2 AT RAMS
SEP 17 × 1:05 PM × FOX

 WK 3 VS GIANTS
SEP 21 × 5:15 PM × PRIME VIDEO

 WK 4 VS CARDINALS
OCT 1 × 1:25 PM × FOX

 WK 5 VS COWBOYS
OCT 8 × 5:20 PM × NBC

 WK 6 AT BROWNS
OCT 15 × 10:00 AM × FOX

 WK 7 AT VIKINGS
OCT 23 × 5:15 PM × ESPN

 WK 8 VS BENGALS
OCT 29 × 1:25 PM × CBS

 WK 9 BYE WEEK

 WK 10 AT JAGUARS
NOV 12 × 10:00 AM × FOX

 WK 11 VS BUCCANEERS
NOV 19 × 1:05 PM × FOX

 WK 12 AT SEAHAWKS
NOV 23 × 5:20 PM × NBC

 WK 13 AT EAGLES
DEC 3 × 1:25 PM × FOX

 WK 14 VS SEAHAWKS
DEC 10 × 1:05 PM × FOX

 WK 15 AT CARDINALS
DEC 17 × 1:05 PM × CBS

 WK 16 VS RAVENS
DEC 25 × 5:15 PM × ABC

 WK 17 AT COMMANDERS
DEC 31 × 10:00 AM × FOX

 WK 18 VS RAMS
TBD

 HOME AWAY

Running Wild with Lock & Co. - A Fantasy Football Odyssey

Hey there, NFL aficionados! Let's dive into the wild world of the Seattle Seahawks. These guys are all about running the ball, and at the helm is the young gun, quarterback Drew Lock. He's not just an arm — he's got wheels that'll keep defenses on their toes.

Meet Rashaad Penny, the muscle behind their ground game. He charges through tackles and catches passes like a pro. On the flip side, we've got the aerial show led by DK Metcalf and Tyler Lockett. Metcalf's the deep threat, and Lockett's the clutch catcher.

Seahawks' game plan? Rule the clock and keep rivals off the field. Run-heavy, with Lock's legs in the spotlight. Quick passes and trick plays, that's their jam.

For your fantasy league, check these studs:

- Drew Lock: A QB with serious upside, surrounded by talent.
- Rashaad Penny: Tackle-breaking running back for your roster.
- DK Metcalf: A touchdown threat with every catch.
- Tyler Lockett: The clutch receiver you need.

Now, check out this nifty chart of their 2022 run-pass habits:

Play Type	Percentage
Passing plays	50.6%
Rushing plays	49.4%

Look at that, nearly 50-50 between passing and running! They love pounding the ground, and their running game is solid. Drew Lock's still settling in, and the O-line's holding its ground.

Expect more of the same in 2023 under new coach Shane Waldron, a run-loving guru. These Seahawks are ready to rumble and keep the clock ticking. Stay tuned!

Key Additions & New Contracts

Player	Position	Contract	Key Addition/New Contract	Impact on Team
Davante Adams	WR	5 years, $141.25 million	Key Addition	Adams is one of the best receivers in the NFL, and he will give the Seahawks a major weapon on offense.
Tyrann Mathieu	S	3 years, $42 million	Key Addition	Mathieu is a versatile safety who can play multiple positions. He will help to solidify the Seahawks' secondary.
Gerald Everett	TE	1 year, $6 million	New Contract	Everett is a good receiving tight end who can also block. He will help to replace Will Dissly, who is a free agent.
Dre'Mont Jones	DE	3 years, $45 million	New Contract	Jones is a good pass rusher who can help to improve the Seahawks' defense.
Jeremiah O'Shaughnessy	C	1 year, $3 million	New Contract	O'Shaughnessy is a good backup center who can also play guard. He will provide depth on the Seahawks' offensive line.

NFL Draft 2023

Round	Pick	Position	College	Player	NFL Fantasy Projection
1	5	WR	Ohio State	Jaxon Smith-Njigba	100
2	37	EDGE	Auburn	Derick Hall	90
3	72	CB	Mississippi State	Martin Emerson	80
4	105	RB	Georgia	Zamir White	70
5	168	OG	Kentucky	Darian Kinnard	60

Key Losses

Position	Player
Cornerback	Sidney Jones
Defensive end	Carlos Dunlap
Offensive tackle	Duane Brown
Wide receiver	Tyler Lockett
Tight end	Gerald Everett

Position	Player	Why chosen
QB	Drew Lock	2nd year player with starting experience
WR	Garrett Wilson	Big-play receiver who can stretch the field
WR	Drake London	Physical receiver who can win contested catches
TE	Treylon Burks	All-around tight end who can block and catch
OT	Charles Cross	Top-rated offensive tackle in the draft
EDGE	Jermaine Johnson II	Pass rusher with the potential to be a difference-maker

SEA '23

2023 REGULAR SEASON SCHEDULE

HOME ↗ ↙ AWAY

SEPT 10 — 1:25PM
WK 1

SEPT 17 — 10:00AM
WK 2

SEPT 24 — 1:05PM
WK 3

OCT 2 — 5:15PM **MNF**
WK 4

BYE WK !!

OCT 15 — 10:00AM
WK 6

OCT 22 — 1:05PM
WK 7

OCT 29 — 1:05PM
WK 8

NOV 5 — 10:00AM
WK 9

NOV 12 — 1:25PM
WK 10

NOV 19 — 1:25PM
WK 11

NOV 23 — 5:20PM
WK 12 — THANKSGIVING

NOV 30 — 5:15PM **TNF**
WK 13

DEC 10 — 1:05PM
WK 14

DEC 17 — 1:25PM
WK 15

DEC 24 — 10:00AM
WK 16

DEC 31 — 1:05PM
WK 17

TBD — TBD
WK 18

All About That Pass Game with the Brady Magic

TAMPA BAY BUCCANEERS

Let's talk Bucs. Tom Brady's leading the charge here, and let's face it, he's a living legend. He's got a knack for both tossing that pigskin and sneaking in a run when you least expect it.

Brady's got some solid backup with a crew of talented receivers. Mike Evans and Chris Godwin are the names to remember. Evans? Touchdown threat. Godwin? The guy who can weave through traffic like a pro.

Don't think they forgot the ground game though. Leonard Fournette's the muscle in the running game, smashing through tackles and snagging catches like a boss.

Their motto? Win by scoring and clock control. They mix it up with passes and runs, while keeping their D on point.

Check out this quick peek into their playbook from 2022:

Play Type	Percentage
Passing plays	61.4%
Rushing plays	38.6%

See that? They love slinging that ball around, more than the league average. Running? Not their strongest suit, but they still managed a decent 129.7 yards per game.

Why the air show?
1. They got killer receivers.
2. Tom Brady's got that golden arm.
3. O-line's solid, only 34 sacks in 2022.

2023? Brace yourselves, Bucs fans. With new coach Todd Bowles in the mix, their pass game might even level up. Stay tuned, and let's see how the story unfolds!

Key Additions & New Contracts

Player	Position	Contract	Key Addition/New Contract	Impact on Team
Russell Gage	Wide Receiver	3 years, $30 million	Key Addition	Gage is a big-play receiver who can stretch the field. He should give the Buccaneers a much-needed boost in their passing game.
Logan Ryan	Cornerback	1 year, $10 million	Key Addition	Ryan is a veteran cornerback who can play both in the slot and on the outside. He should help improve the Buccaneers' secondary.
Carlton Davis	Cornerback	3 years, $50.5 million	New Contract	Davis is a young, talented cornerback who is one of the best in the NFL. He is getting a big payday, but he is worth it.

Key Losses

Position	Player
Defensive tackle	Ndamukong Suh
Cornerback	Sean Murphy-Bunting
Safety	Jordan Whitehead
Wide receiver	Chris Godwin
Offensive tackle	Donovan Smith

NFL Draft 2023

Round	Pick	Position	College	Player	NFL Fantasy Projection
1	19	DT	Pitt	Calijah Kancey	120
2	50	EDGE	Louisville	YaYa Diaby	110
3	82	TE	Purdue	Payne Durham	90
4	134	OG	Indiana	Matt Waletzko	100
5	171	WR	Nebraska	Samori Toure	80
6	181	CB	Kansas State	Malik Knowles	70
6	214	S	Georgia	Lewis Cine	60

Position	Player	Reason
QB	Kyle Trask	The Buccaneers need to find a long-term successor to Tom Brady, and Trask could be that guy. He has the talent and potential to be a franchise quarterback.
WR	Tyler Johnson	Johnson is a good deep threat who can stretch the field. He could be a valuable weapon for the Buccaneers' offense.
WR	Jaelon Darden	Darden is a good slot receiver who can make plays after the catch. He could be a valuable asset in the Buccaneers' short-yardage offense.
OL	Luke Goedeke	Goedeke is a good run blocker who can develop into a starting offensive tackle.
TE	Cade Otton	Otton is a good receiving tight end who can block. He could be a valuable target for the Buccaneers' quarterback.

TAMPA BAY BUCCANEERS 2023 SCHEDULE

PRESEASON

	P1 Pittsburgh Steelers	Friday	8/11	7:00 PM	News Channel 8 HD
	P2 @ New York Jets	Saturday	8/19	7:30 PM	News Channel 8 HD
	P3 Baltimore Ravens	Saturday	8/26	7:00 PM	News Channel 8 HD

REGULAR SEASON

	WK1 @ Minnesota Vikings	Sunday	9/10	1:00 PM	CBS
	WK2 Chicago Bears	Sunday	9/17	1:00 PM	FOX
	WK3 Philadelphia Eagles	Monday	9/25	7:15 PM	abc
	WK4 @ New Orleans Saints	Sunday	10/1	1:00 PM	FOX

BYE WEEK

	WK6 Detroit Lions	Sunday	10/15	1:00 PM	FOX
	WK7 Atlanta Falcons	Sunday	10/22	1:00 PM	FOX
	WK8 @ Buffalo Bills	Thursday	10/26	8:15 PM	prime video
	WK9 @ Houston Texans	Sunday	11/5	1:00 PM	CBS
	WK10 Tennessee Titans	Sunday	11/12	1:00 PM	CBS
	WK11 @ San Francisco 49ers	Sunday	11/19	4:05 PM	FOX
	WK12 @ Indianapolis Colts	Sunday	11/26	1:00 PM	CBS
	WK13 Carolina Panthers	Sunday	12/3	1:00 PM	CBS
	WK14 @ Atlanta Falcons	Sunday	12/10	1:00 PM	CBS
	WK15 @ Green Bay Packers	Sunday	12/17	1:00 PM	FOX
	WK16 Jacksonville Jaguars	Sunday	12/24	4:05 PM	CBS
	WK17 New Orleans Saints	Sunday	12/31	1:00 PM	FOX
	WK18 @ Carolina Panthers	TBA	TBA	TBA	

HOME   **AWAY**

ALL TIMES EASTERN. DATES AND TIMES SUBJECT TO CHANGE.
SIMULCAST AVAILABLE ON NFL NETWORK AND AMAZON, SUBJECT TO CHANGE.

Run Game Strong, Derrick Henry's the Man!

Get ready, Titans fans! The Titans march to the beat of Derrick Henry's thunderous run-game. He's a force to be reckoned with, a touchdown threat every time he gets that ball in his hands.

Ryan Tannehill, the Titans' quarterback, keeps the passing game solid. He's got the arm, but he's not as nimble as Henry on his feet.

The Titans love to hog the clock and keep rivals off the field by pounding the run and rock-solid defense.

They've cooked up schemes to capitalize on Henry's might, using power plays and sneaky passes. Quick throws spread the magic to their playmakers too.

Picture this: your fantasy squad with these key players:

- Derrick Henry: Must-have. Beast of a running back, scores galore.
- Ryan Tannehill: Your QB solution with a cannon arm.
- A.J. Brown: Unleashes chaos on opposing defenses.

Check out the 2022 run-pass mix for Titans:

Play Type	Percentage
Passing plays	48.8%
Rushing plays	51.2%

Titans bucked the trend by favoring the run more than the league average of 45.4%. They averaged 143.3 rushing yards and 224.8 passing yards per game.

Why did they run wild?

- Derrick Henry's powerhouse presence.
- Solid offensive line (28 sacks in 2022, 16th lowest in NFL).
- Tannehill's more of a pocket-passer.

Hold onto your hats, 'cause Titans' run-pass game is likely to keep its groove in 2023. New coach Todd Downing loves ground and pound, especially if health cooperates. Game on!

Key Additions & New Contracts

Player	Position	Contract	Key Addition/New Contract	Impact on Team
Arden Key	OLB	3 years, $29 million	New Contract	Key pass rusher to help improve the Titans' defense.
Andre Dillard	OT	1 year, $1.198 million	Free Agent Signing	Depth offensive tackle to compete for a starting job.
Azeez Al-Shaair	LB	3 years, $24 million	New Contract	Solid linebacker who can play multiple positions.
Treylon Burks	WR	4 years, $25 million	Draft Pick	Big-play receiver who can stretch the field.

Key Losses

Position	Player
Wide receiver	AJ Brown
Edge rusher	Harold Landry
Safety	Kevin Byard
Cornerback	Caleb Farley
Guard	Rodger Saffold

NFL Draft 2023

Round	Pick	Position	College	Player	NFL Fantasy Projection
1	11	OT	Northwestern	Peter Skoronski	90
2	33	QB	Kentucky	Will Levis	100
3	81	RB	Tulane	Tyjae Spears	80
5	147	TE	Cincinnati	Josh Whyle	70
6	186	OT	Maryland	Jaelyn Duncan	60

Position	Player	Explanation
QB	Malik Willis	The Titans need a long-term answer at quarterback, and Willis has the potential to be that guy. He is a mobile quarterback with a strong arm.
WR	Treylon Burks	The Titans need a big-play receiver, and Burks fits the bill. He is 6'3" and 225 pounds, and he can make plays down the field.
OT	Bernhard Raimann	The Titans need to protect their quarterback, and Raimann is a good pass blocker. He is also athletic enough to play in space.
EDGE	Boye Mafe	The Titans need to get more pressure on the quarterback, and Mafe is a good pass rusher. He is quick and has a good first step.
DT	DeMarvin Leal	The Titans need to improve their run defense, and Leal is a good run stopper. He is also athletic enough to get after the quarterback.
LB	Nakobe Dean	The Titans need a leader on defense, and Dean is a good candidate. He is a hard-nosed player who is always around the ball.

2023 SEASON SCHEDULE

AUG. 12	AUG. 19	AUG. 25
PS 1—AT	PS 2—AT	PS 3—VS
CHI	**MIN**	**NE**
12 PM	7 PM	7:15 PM

SEP. 10	SEP. 17	OCT. 1
WEEK 1—AT	WEEK 2—VS	WEEK 4—VS
NO	**LAC**	**CIN**
12 PM	12 PM	12 PM

OCT. 8	OCT. 15	OCT. 29
WEEK 5—AT	WEEK 6—VS	WEEK 8—VS
IND	**BAL**	**ATL**
12 PM	8:30 AM	12 PM
	LONDON	

NOV. 2	NOV. 12	NOV. 26
WEEK 9—AT	WEEK 10—AT	WEEK 12—VS
PIT	**TB**	**CAR**
7:15 PM	12 PM	12 PM
TNF		

DEC. 3	DEC. 11	DEC. 17	DEC. 24
WEEK 13—VS	WEEK 14—AT	WEEK 15—VS	WEEK 16—VS
IND	**MIA**	**HOU**	**SEA**
12 PM	7:15 PM	12 PM	12 PM
	MNF		

DEC. 31	TBD
WEEK 17—AT	WEEK 18—VS
HOU	**JAX**
12 PM	TBD

WEEK 7
BYE

HOME | AWAY

ALL TIMES LISTED ARE CENTRAL TIME ZONE (CT)

PRESENTED BY
SEATGEEK

WASHINGTON COMMANDERS

Run-First Strategy with a Sprinkle of Young Quarterback Promise

Let's talk Commanders! They're all about that run game, and leading the charge is quarterback Carson Wentz. He's not just a passer, oh no, he's got some slick run moves up his sleeves that leave defenses scratching their heads.

On the run front, they've got Antonio Gibson, a powerhouse of a running back. He bulldozes through tackles and can snag catches like a boss.

But wait, there's more! Their passing game stars Terry McLaurin. This dude is like a bolt of lightning on the field, zipping past defenders.

Now, their game plan? It's like a delicious cake recipe—control that clock and starve the other guys of the ball. How? By running like there's no tomorrow and playing some solid D.

Their playbook is all about Carson's run prowess. They throw in zone runs and trick passes to let him do his thing. Quick throws? You betcha! Get the ball to their stars and watch the magic happen.

Bottom line: Commanders are all about that run life, with Carson Wentz leading the charge. They want that clock on their side, ready to snatch those victories.

Now, meet some fantasy gems from their crew:

- Carson Wentz: If you're a fantasy quarterback gambler, he's your man. With running and throwing skills, he's backed by solid teammates.
- Antonio Gibson: If your team craves a tough runner, Gibson's the answer.
- Terry McLaurin: You want a receiver that's a game-changer? Say hello to McLaurin, your guy.

And now, drum roll, please! Behold, the Washington Commanders' run-pass flavors from 2022:

Play Type	Percentage
Passing plays	48.8%
Rushing plays	51.2%

They're all about the run, as you can see, a touch above the league average. 2022 showed their run game power, averaging 195.6 rushing yards and 220.6 passing yards per game.

"Why the run, you ask?" Well, reasons galore:

- A beastly duo of running backs, Antonio Gibson and J.D. McKissic.
- Carson Wentz's growth story continues.
- A sturdy offensive line with only 33 sacks allowed in 2022, ranking 14th in the NFL.

What's cooking for 2023? Well, their new head coach, Martin Mayhew, is known for a hearty run game. Brace yourselves for more run magic, especially if injuries stay at bay."

Key Additions & New Contracts

Player	Position	Contract	Key Addition/New Contract	Impact on Team
Marcus Williams	Safety	5 years, $70 million	Key Addition	Williams is a top-tier safety who will help to solidify the Commanders' secondary.
Daron Payne	Defensive tackle	3 years, $40 million	New Contract	Payne is a good defensive tackle who will help to improve the Commanders' run defense.
Dustin Hopkins	Kicker	3 years, $12 million	New Contract	Hopkins is a reliable kicker who will help to stabilize the Commanders' kicking game.
Terry McLaurin	Wide receiver	3 years, $71 million	Key Addition	McLaurin is a star wide receiver who will help to keep the Commanders' passing game dangerous.
Cade Otton	Tight end	4 years, $3.5 million	Key Addition	Otton is a talented tight end who will help to improve the Commanders' passing game.

Key Losses

Position	Player
Offensive Tackle	Brandon Scherff
Defensive Tackle	Tim Settle
Cornerback	William Jackson III
Safety	Landon Collins

NFL Draft 2023

Round	Pick	Position	College	Player	NFL Fantasy Projection
1	16	OT	Mississippi State	Charles Cross	90
2	47	CB	Illinois	Kyler Gordon	80
3	97	C	Arkansas	Ricky Stromberg	70
4	118	G	Utah	Olusegun Oluwatimi	60
5	163	EDGE	Penn State	Arnold Ebiketie	50

Pos	Player	Why chosen
QB	Carson Wentz	Wentz is the starting quarterback and he is under contract for two more seasons.
WR	Terry McLaurin	McLaurin is a star wide receiver and he is under contract for three more seasons.
LT	Charles Cross	Cross is a good pass blocker and he has the potential to be a franchise left tackle.
CB	Kyler Gordon	Gordon is a good cover corner and he has the potential to be a starter in the Commanders' secondary.
EDGE	Arnold Ebiketie	Ebiketie is a good pass rusher and he has the potential to be a difference-maker in the Commanders' defense.

2023 W SCHEDULE

WEEK	DAY	DATE	OPPONENT	TIME (ET)
1	**Sunday**	**September 10**	**Arizona Cardinals**	**1:00 PM**
2	Sunday	September 17	@ Denver Broncos	4:25 PM
3	**Sunday**	**September 24**	**Buffalo Bills**	**1:00 PM**
4	Sunday	October 1	@ Philadelphia Eagles	1:00 PM
5	**Thursday**	**October 5**	**Chicago Bears**	**8:15 PM**
6	Sunday	October 15	@ Atlanta Falcons	1:00 PM
7	Sunday	October 22	@ New York Giants	1:00 PM
8	**Sunday**	**October 29**	**Philadelphia Eagles**	**1:00 PM**
9	Sunday	November 5	@ New England Patriots	1:00 PM
10	Sunday	November 12	@ Seattle Seahawks	4:25 PM
11	**Sunday**	**November 19**	**New York Giants**	**1:00 PM**
12	Thursday	November 23	@ Dallas Cowboys	4:30 PM
13	**Sunday**	**December 3**	**Miami Dolphins**	**1:00 PM**
14	N/A	N/A	BYE WEEK	N/A
15	Sunday	December 17	@ Los Angeles Rams	4:05 PM
16	Sunday	December 24	@ New York Jets	1:00 PM
17	**Sunday**	**December 31**	**San Francisco 49ers**	**1:00 PM**
18	**TBD**	**TBD**	**Dallas Cowboys**	**TBD***

Home Games are in **Bold** | *Schedule Subject to Change

Basic Elements

The essence of success lies in securing players who outshine their price tag. Football's canvas isn't painted with formulas, it's a symphony of averages—receptions, yards, touches. Hunt down players destined to surpass these benchmarks, ignited by an opponent's injury or game dynamics. The alchemy of exemplary outlook lies in exploiting opponents' vulnerabilities, capitalizing on game flow, or sailing on the crest of high point totals. Let's demystify the distinction between value and cheap—the former reaps higher dividends than anticipated. Rob Gronkowski and Andrew Luck might stage value shows some weeks.

Upside: The tryst with potential, unsullied by price. This realm orbits touchdowns, glimmers of triumph at Draft Kings. Cash game upside unveils through stable, middle-high tier players in golden circumstances. Tournament upside, a mercurial dance, stars low-mid tier contenders, basking in uncharted waters of high-potential scores.

Safety: Often obscured by the dazzle of upside, safety shines bright in cash game lineups. In this tapestry, efficiency and volume reign. Roddy White, Frank Gore, Jason Witten, and their ilk personify this reliability, weaving tales of consistency. Enter quarterbacks—paragons of safety. Andrew Luck, Aaron Rodgers command a premium, while fleet-footed Russell Wilson grants a budget-friendly refuge. Rushing prowess transforms them into guardians of floor and fantasy points.

Brace yourself for a voyage through the labyrinth of fantasy football's core—an art where value, upside, and safety weave a tapestry of triumph and strategy.

Assembling all the pieces

In the tapestry of daily fantasy football, safety wields both its merits and perils. Embrace a core of security with a 75% safe lineup for cash games, tapering it to 30-40% in tourneys. But don't be beguiled by the siren's call of extravagance. The art of outpacing hinges on more than audacity. Yield not to the allure of the highest-paid, instead, seek data's counsel, leading you to the diamond in the rough, the opponent's soft underbelly basking in your player's prowess.

Harness the power of players riding high on upside and floors, balancing with sound value choices. Behold matchups and the whims of game flow dictating performers who outshine their summative statistics. When courting quarterbacks of caliber, seek affordable talents propelling their offensive orchestra, conducting a high-scoring symphony. The pages of history and a favorable dance card with fate should underscore their NFL triumphs.

Yet, beware the mirage of unrealistic hopes from a budget-friendly backup. Although expecting Rodgers or Luck-level brilliance is folly, a fraction of their price yields dividends. Yet ponder this, if you shun a premium quarterback to elevate Le'Veon Bell over a rival like Seattle or Buffalo, do you truly harvest the full bounty of your investment? Remember, a mid-to-high-tier quarterback overthrows the likes of Cassel, Mallet, or Keenum.

Amidst the gridiron's chaos, emerges ProFootballFocus' gift, the "Elusive Rating," gauging a rusher's prowess in conjuring something from nothing. Bell, Lynch, and Lacy surge skyward on this spectrum, while Ivory defies expectations. Their mastery births big plays—100-yard escapades and touchdown anthems. In the symphony of big plays, wideouts lead the charge, threefold more than tight ends and backs combined. T.Y. Hilton, DeSean Jackson, and Mike Evans are the virtuosos of this symphony, their clarion calls echoing 20 yards downfield.

So, fellow gridiron enthusiasts, the art of daily fantasy marries strategy and serendipity, demanding tactical finesse to render the symphony of triumph. Let the gridiron tales spin, your fantasy feats bloom, and the echoes of your wise choices resound through the hallowed halls of football lore.

Printed in Great Britain
by Amazon

29487866R00064